Beatrice

Goes To

Brighton

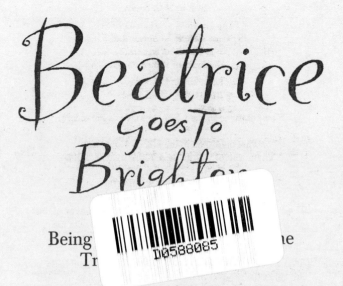

Being the ... ...he
Tr...

M. C. BEATON

Constable & Robinson Ltd
3 The Lanchesters
162 Fulham Palace Road
London W6 9ER
www.constablerobinson.com

First published in the US by St Martin's Press, 1991

First published in the UK by Robinson,
an imprint of Constable & Robinson Ltd, 2011

Copyright © M.C. Beaton 1991

The right of M.C. Beaton to be identified as the author of this
work has been asserted by her in accordance with the
Copyright, Designs and Patents Act 1988

A copy of the British Library Cataloguing in
Publication data is available from the British Library

ISBN: 978-1-84901-482-3

Typeset by TW Typesetting, Plymouth, Devon

Printed and bound in the EU

3 5 7 9 10 8 6 4 2

1

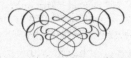

Then dress, then dinner, then awakes the world!
Then glare the lamps, then whirl the wheels, then roar
Throughout street and square fast flashing chariots, hurled
Like harnessed meteors.

Lord Byron

Lady Beatrice Marsham had been a widow for over a year and enjoyed every minute of her now single state. She well remembered the first day of her freedom, when she had descended the stairs of her husband's town house to see her spouse, Mr Harry Blackstone, being carried into the hall by his drinking companions.

'Foxed again,' they had called cheerfully, dumping the body in a chair. Lady Beatrice had looked at her husband with impatient distaste, called her maid, pulled on her gloves, and gone out to make various calls.

1

She was surprised on her return to find the blinds down and a hatchment over the door. Her husband, it transpired, was not dead drunk, but simply dead.

As Lady Beatrice – she had never used her married name – settled herself comfortably in a corner seat of the Brighton stage-coach, she remembered her overwhelming feeling of relief when they told her Harry was dead. No more drunken scenes, no more embarrassing fumblings in the bedchamber at night, no more jealous rages. She was free of it all.

Her parents, the Earl and Countess of Debren, had arranged that marriage. Lady Beatrice had assumed that, being a widow of twenty-eight, she would now be left alone. But only two days ago, her father had visited her to say that a marriage had been arranged for her with Sir Geoffrey Handford. In vain had she raged. The earl had pointed out brutally that she had not yet borne any sons. It was her duty to marry again. Then Sir Geoffrey had called, a thickset, brutish man in snuff-stained clothes.

To get rid of both her father and Sir Geoffrey, Lady Beatrice had said she would consider the matter and had then decided to take herself off to Brighton, hoping that by the time she returned, the matter would have been forgotten. She had sent her servants and most of her baggage ahead, having rented a house in Brighton through an agent in London. She had planned to drive down the Brighton road herself, for she was an expert whip, but the weather had turned very wet and so she had decided to take the stage.

It was not unusual for an aristocrat, even a female one, to travel on the Brighton stage. The stage-coaches on that route were becoming very fashionable. Had not the Prince of Wales made Brighton fashionable? And it therefore followed that everything associated with that watering-place should be considered bon ton. Besides, the Brighton road was famous for its inns, and the journey took a mere six hours.

Also, it was amusing to be in such a plebeian carriage and in such low company. Lady Beatrice was an expert at keeping low company at bay. In fact, she had become quite expert at keeping the whole wide world at bay. She had been in love once, when she was eighteen, a tremulous, vulnerable maiden. That was when her parents had betrothed her to Harry. She felt that by that act they had taken everything from her, her hopes, her innocence, and, most of all, her freedom. She grew in beauty and coldness. She despised all men. She occasionally amused herself with flirting with one of the beasts, only to reject him as nastily as she knew how.

She wished the coach would move. It was Sunday, and everything in London was shuttered and closed and sooty and black. All the church bells were ringing, a persistent, irritating cacophony. Not far from the White Bear Inn in Piccadilly was St James's Church, which, reflected Lady Beatrice sourly, seemed to have a more hellish group of bell-ringers than most as they performed their jangly, insistent triples and majors. What did the workers of the world, after toiling six miserable days a week, think of this day of rest, black and more miserable than all the others, dingy and stale and dull? thought Lady Beatrice. How could one think of spiritual things when no prospect pleased and the air was rent by the clamour of the bells?

She glanced briefly at her fellow passengers. Beside her was a small dumpy man who smelled strongly of ale, and beside him in the other corner was a tired, bedraggled woman with a snivelling child on her lap. Across from her was a soldier, asleep with his mouth open; beside him, a small dwarf of a woman with huge pale eyes like saucers, and opposite Lady Beatrice was a thin lady, elegantly dressed. She had sandy hair under a neat bonnet, a crooked nose, odd eyes which appeared to change colour, and a clever mouth. Lady Beatrice's chilly gaze rested a bit longer on this lady than it had done on the others. To her surprise, the lady smiled and said, 'Allow me to introduce myself. I am Miss Hannah Pym of London.'

Lady Beatrice allowed her eyelids to droop slightly, her upper lip to raise a fraction, and then she slowly turned her head away and looked out of the window.

Miss Hannah Pym bit her lip in mortification. Although Hannah now had the appearance, clothes, manner, and speech of a lady, inside lurked the servant she all too recently had been, and she thought the cold and beautiful creature opposite had snubbed her because she had recognized in Hannah an inferior person.

She covertly studied the haughty lady. Lady Beatrice had jet-black hair under a Lavinia bonnet, her face shadowed by the wide brim. She had very clear white skin, a straight nose, and large grey eyes fringed with thick lashes. Her mouth was slightly pinched at the corners, as if it had once been a fuller mouth which the years and disappointment had thinned down. Hannah sensed that she was tired and anxious, and yet Hannah was disproportionately worried by that snub, if snub it had been.

Her legacy of five thousand pounds, left her by her late employer, Mr Clarence, in his will, had initially seemed a vast sum, but now that she had become accustomed to higher society in the shape of Mr Clarence's brother, Sir George, who had recently taken her out to the opera, and since she had moved her quarters to the fashionable West End, it seemed very little in a world where men and women gambled more than that at the gaming tables of St James's every night.

And yet, just a little while ago, she had been Hannah Pym of Thornton Hall in Kensington, a housekeeper who had clawed her way up the servants' hierarchy from scullery maid.

Her thoughts drifted back over the years. She should not despise her old life. She had been well-treated, particularly by pretty Mrs Clarence before she had run off with that footman and left her husband to sink into apathy. The hard times had come when Mr Clarence had become a semi-recluse, locking up half the rooms and dismissing half the servants, and there were no more balls or parties. That was when Hannah had begun to watch the stage-coaches, or Flying Machines as they were called, hurtle along the road at the end of the estate, symbols of freedom and adventure.

This was to be her fourth journey. The past three had been full of adventure. She sighed a little. She was a determined matchmaker and there was no one on this coach she could possibly pair together in her mind. Her footman was on the roof with the outside passengers. Hannah brightened. It surely increased her social standing to have a footman. She had adopted her deaf-and-dumb footman, Benjamin, during her last adventurous journey. He expressly did not want wages. In fact, he had an embarrassing habit of paying her out of his frequent winnings at dice.

The chilly lady opposite turned her gaze on Hannah again. Hannah immediately said airily, 'I do hope my poor footman is not getting a soaking up on the roof.'

A slight look of contempt flicked across the fine eyes opposite. Hannah cursed herself and wished she had never spoken. Only parvenus spoke of having footmen. The frigid travelling companion she was trying to impress probably had scores of footmen.

Worse was to come. The small dwarf-like woman next to Hannah said in a hoarse whisper, 'Ain't no use tryin' to impress the likes o' her. She don't care a fig for any of us.'

'I was not trying to impress,' said Hannah with a pathetic attempt at hauteur.

The guard on the roof blew a fanfare and the coach rumbled forward.

The coach was to take the new route to Brighton, going by Croydon, Merstham, Reigate, Crawley and Cuckfield, making the distance fifty-three miles exactly.

Hannah looked bleakly out at the driving rain and decided to ignore that cold creature opposite. She should, after all, be looking forward to her first visit to Brighton.

The Prince of Wales had gone to the fishing village, then called Brighthelmstone, as early as 1783 to try a sea-water cure for swollen glands. He rented a small farmhouse on the Steyne, a broad strip of lawn that ran down to the sea. In the summer of 1787, Henry Holland, fresh from planning the reconstruction of Carlton House, built for the prince a bow-fronted house in the classical manner, topped by a shallow dome, which came to be known as the Prince of Wales's Marine Pavilion. The prince, who had a taste for oriental design, was rumoured to want to create an oriental palace for himself. He wanted to enclose the entire pavilion in the style of a Chinese pagoda, but so far had been held in check when it was pointed out that such a design would clash with Holland's classicism.

Hannah had hopes of actually seeing the prince, for he was reported to be in Brighton, and although he longed for privacy and hated the London mob, he was more tolerant of the people who flocked after him to Brighton to stare, some of them armed with opera glasses and even telescopes.

Lady Beatrice was beginning to feel oddly uncomfortable. There had been no reason to be so rude to the lady opposite. Hannah, could she have known, would have been delighted to learn that she was classed in Lady Beatrice's mind as 'lady', rather than 'woman'.

And yet Lady Beatrice was used to cutting all and sundry. She had no female friends, finding the ladies she met at balls and parties too silly and affected. Although she was dimly aware that she had taken her own misery over her marriage out on everyone else, she had felt more comfortable in her isolation, using her beauty to attract men for the fun of repulsing them.

It must be, reflected Lady Beatrice, because her companion of the stage-coach opposite had such an expressive face. For the first time in years, she would put herself in the way of a snub in order to make amends. Lady Beatrice smiled slightly at Hannah and said, 'Dreadful weather, is it not?'

Now, here was Hannah's opportunity, and for the life of her, she could not take it. She started by turning her head away, only to be made aware of the avid stare of those pale, saucer-like eyes next to her. She turned back to face Lady Beatrice. 'Yes, quite dreadful,' she said calmly.

Then she took a small book out of her reticule and pretended to read.

The coach drew up at the Bear in Croydon to change horses. The passengers filed into the inn for cakes and tea because it was in that meal-less desert between breakfast, which was usually about nine in the morning, and dinner, normally at four in the afternoon, although some fashionables were already beginning to take their dinner at a later hour.

Hannah was pleased she had her footman, Benjamin, so tall and well-groomed, with his clever East End face, in attendance, well aware of the air of consequence it gave her. Hannah often wondered where Benjamin had come from. She had been instrumental in rescuing Benjamin from the gallows for a crime he had not committed, and he had become her devoted slave. Although he was deaf and dumb, he could write, but he never wrote down for Hannah any of his history. But he had come a long way in appearance from the battered-looking criminal in irons who had touched Hannah's heart on her last stage-coach journey. He wore his plush livery with an air, his hair powdered, his white gloves impeccable.

There was a small altercation when the woman with the pale eyes, who had announced to all in general that she was Mrs Hick, pulled a large plate of cakes in front of her and began to demolish them. The woman with the child glared and pointed out that there were others at the table who might like cakes, and her child began to roar and cry as he saw all the treats disappearing down the little woman's large mouth.

Benjamin walked firmly round the table, snatched up the plate of cakes, presented them first to Hannah, then to everyone else, and then set the remainder back down on the table as far away from Mrs Hick as possible.

'You are fortunate in having such an efficient servant,' said Lady Beatrice to Hannah.

'Yes,' said Hannah baldly, having not quite forgiven her for that snub.

'Do you travel all the way to Brighton?' pursued Lady Beatrice.

'Yes,' said Hannah, and visibly thawing, added, 'I am looking forward to seeing the sea again.'

'And that is the sole reason for your journey?' Lady Beatrice looked amused.

'Not quite, Miss . . . er . . .'

Lady Beatrice took out a card-case and extracted a card and handed it to Hannah. Hannah coloured. She herself had no cards.

To her surprise, Benjamin leaned over her shoulder and put a small leather case down in front of her. Hannah opened it and saw in amazement that it contained elegantly engraved cards. 'Miss Hannah Pym, 16 South Audley Street, London'.

She quietly took one out and presented it to Lady Beatrice, determined to ask Benjamin later how he had come by them.

'So, my lady,' said Hannah, 'what takes you to Brighton?'

'I have rented a house there,' said Lady Beatrice. 'London fatigues me.'

'I do not think I could ever tire of London,' said Hannah. Her odd eyes glowed. 'But I love to travel. I have had so many adventures.'

'Stage-coach travel can be adventurous,' said Lady Beatrice drily. 'Broken poles, bolting horses, coaches stuck in ruts or snowstorms, not to mention highwaymen.'

'Oh, I've had highwaymen,' said Hannah proudly, and with the air of a professional invalid saying, 'Oh, yes, I have had the smallpox.'

Lady Beatrice laughed, and that laugh quite altered her appearance. The eyes shone and that tight mouth relaxed and became fuller. 'I see you are an intrepid traveller, Miss Pym.'

'And matchmaker,' boasted Hannah. 'I have been instrumental in making matches between stage-coach passengers . . .'

Her voice faded away. A shutter had come down over Lady Beatrice's eyes.

'I see we are leaving,' said Lady Beatrice. She rose quickly and walked out into the inn yard. Hannah followed, sad that her boast of matchmaking had had the effect of freezing this strange Lady Beatrice up again. And then, as Hannah reached the inn door, she saw a strange sight. A handsome travelling carriage was standing in the yard with the coachman on the box and two grooms on the backstrap. There were also two outriders.

A thickset man approached Lady Beatrice and seized her by the arm. She let out a cry. He bent and said something, and Hannah, watching, startled, was sure that he was thrusting something like a pistol or a knife against Lady Beatrice's side.

She ran forward, with Benjamin at her heels. 'Lady Beatrice!' called Hannah. 'Is aught amiss?'

The thickset man glared at her and said, 'Lady Beatrice has decided to continue the journey in the comfort of my carriage. Is that not so, my dear?'

Lady Beatrice was very white. 'That is so,' she said in a low voice.

The man who held her so tightly called to one of the grooms, 'Fetch my lady's baggage from the coach.' He then guided Lady Beatrice into his own carriage, climbed in after her and slammed the door.

'Help!' shouted Hannah at the top of her voice. Ostlers, waiters, and the other passengers came running up. 'I am sure Lady Beatrice is being abducted,' said Hannah wildly.

The groom had found Lady Beatrice's baggage in the coach and was returning with the coachman.

'What's all this, then?' demanded the coachman. There was a babble of voices above which Hannah's sounded loud and clear. 'Lady Beatrice is being taken away by force.'

'Ho, now.' The coachman, like most of his kind, was fat and grog-faced and swathed in shawls. He lumbered towards the carriage. The man inside let down the glass.

'Are you running off wiv thet 'ooman?' demanded the coachman.

'Stow your whids, coachee,' growled the man. 'I am merely taking Lady Beatrice to Brighton in a more comfortable carriage.'

'Let her speak for herself,' shouted Mrs Hick.

Lady Beatrice leaned forward. 'I am going of my own free will,' she said quietly.

'That's that, then.' The coachman rounded truculently on the watchers. 'Who started all this 'ere fuss, then? Let's be 'aving ye.'

'It was I,' said Hannah unrepentantly. 'I am sure that man was holding a pistol or a knife to Lady Beatrice's side.'

The coachman turned away in disgust and could be heard to mutter something about women with bats in their belfries who read too many romances.

The other passengers surveyed Hannah reproachfully when they were all on board again.

'Trouble is,' said Mrs Hick, who was now eating a large sandwich, 'you was so taken up wiff the idea of speakin' to one of the nobs, that you got carried away.'

Well, there was one lesson Hannah Pym had learned from Lady Beatrice. She drooped her eyelids wearily, curled her lip, and turned her head away.

'You learned that offa her,' jeered Mrs Hick with all the dreadful perspicacity of some vulgar women and drunks. 'Don't come the 'igh and mighty wiff me. Reckon that so-called footman o' yourn ain't none other than your son.'

This was greeted by a roar of laughter from the other passengers and Hannah felt like the uttermost fool. She felt she was standing astride the yawning gulf of servant and lady with a foot on either side and not knowing quite how to behave.

She settled back and closed her eyes firmly. She thought of Mrs Clarence, her late employer's dainty, pretty wife. Now Mrs Clarence, mused Hannah, had been a real lady. She had treated everyone just the same. 'But she must have had low tastes,' jeered an awful Mrs Hick-like voice in her head, 'or she would never have run off with that footman.' Hannah turned her thoughts to Sir George Clarence. Now *there* was a gentleman! He had even taken her to Gunter's for ices, introduced her to his bank, taken her to the opera.

'But you can never hope for anything else,' sneered that awful voice again. 'I do believe you are getting quite spoony about him, Hannah Pym, and he knew you as a servant.'

Hannah opened her eyes and looked out of the window to banish her thoughts. A watery sunlight was struggling through the clouds. There were wild daffodils blowing by the roadside, dipping and swaying in the blustery wind. Soon the leaves would be back on the trees and there would be summer to look forward to.

The journey continued on in blessed silence, blessed for Hannah, who did not think she could bear any more insults.

But when they arrived in Cuckfield and entered the White Hart, somehow the splendour and elegance of the famous inn brought out the worst in Mrs Hick.

She saw Hannah looking with interest at a tall man who was lounging at his ease in the corner. Hannah was wondering who he was. In an age when most people were not much taller than five feet, he seemed a giant. He had lazy blue, amiable eyes and golden hair, tied back at the nape of his neck with a blue silk ribbon. He had a strong, handsome face, lightly tanned, broad shoulders, and the finest pair of legs Hannah had ever seen. He was wearing a beautifully cut coat of fine blue wool with gold buttons, worn open over a silk waistcoat embroidered with pea-cocks. His legs were encased in skin-tight leather breeches and Hessian boots with jaunty little gold tassels.

Tiny Mrs Hick screwed round in her chair and her saucer-like eyes fastened on the focus of Hannah's attention.

'Miss 'Igh and Mighty 'ere is casting her glims at that prime bit o' Fancy,' jeered Mrs Hick. 'Next, she'll be over there, chattering about 'er footman.'

The waiter, a lofty individual with a sallow face, snickered as he placed another plate of cakes on the table.

'We see 'em all, ma'am,' he said to Mrs Hick. 'You've no idea the number o' ladies who come in on the coach pretending to be Quality.'

Hannah half-rose from her seat, her face scarlet. But a voice from behind her chair made her sink back down in amazement.

'Shut yer bleeding cake-'ole,' said a Cockney voice, 'or I'll draw yer cork, you litre turd ov a jackanapes.'

Hannah twisted round and stared open-mouthed at Benjamin. She was as amazed as if the teapot itself had burst into speech.

'You'll draw my cork,' sneered the waiter. 'I'd like to see you try.'

'Outside,' roared Benjamin.

'The dumb fellow can speak arter all,' cried Mrs Hick.

Benjamin and the waiter marched outside to the inn yard. 'A mill!' cried the soldier, and the whole inn followed them outside, even the aristocratic-looking gentleman, even Hannah, almost as dumb with amazement as Benjamin had pretended to be.

Benjamin carefully removed his coat and placed it on a mounting-block. Bets were rapidly being laid, the betters favouring the waiter. Benjamin then removed his clean shirt and placed that tenderly on top of his coat. Stripped, he revealed a well-muscled chest and strong arms. Some of the bets changed in favour of Benjamin.

Hannah made a move to stop her footman but found her arm taken in a gentle but powerful grasp. She found the aristocrat beside her. 'Don't ruin a fight, ma'am,' he said plaintively. 'I should not really worry about your footman. My money is on him.'

'I didn't know he could talk,' said Hannah. 'All this time and he has pretended to be deaf and dumb.'

The waiter and Benjamin squared up. The coach-man, who had elected himself as referee, dropped the handkerchief and the pair set to.

Benjamin dodged and feinted, moving like light-ning, prancing about on his new leather pumps, which he kept polished like glass.

Then Benjamin's fist seemed to come up from the ground and it smacked the waiter full on the chin with an enormous thwack. There was a silence as the waiter staggered this way and that and then stretched his length on the ground.

In an age when a good fight was expected to last eighteen rounds at least, this was considered a poor sort of match.

Hannah marched up to Benjamin as he carefully donned his shirt.

'What is the meaning of this, Benjamin?' she cried. 'Why did you pretend you couldn't speak?'

Benjamin smoothed down the ruffles of his shirt with a fastidious hand and then put on his plush coat. 'I couldn't tell you, modom,' he said in strangulated accents very different from his Cockney outburst in the inn. 'You was that sorry for me. I pretended to be deaf and dumb, 'cos I knew Lady Carsey liked freaks and I needed work. That's how I got started as a footman.'

'But when Lady Carsey falsely accused you of taking her brooch, why did you not speak then?'

'I daren't, modom, for the magistrate might have thought that since I was lying about one thing, therefore I might be lying about being innocent of the theft. Not that it did me much good.'

'But you had no reason to lie to *me*!'

'Thought you might not be sorry for me no more and turn me off,' mumbled Benjamin.

Hannah, aware of the listeners, said, 'We shall talk of this further when we get to Brighton.'

Lord Alistair Munro watched with amusement as Hannah took her seat with Benjamin standing punctiliously behind her chair.

Mrs Hick had bet on the waiter and was not feeling charitable. 'Fancy not knowing her own footman can speak. That is, if he *is* a footman.'

'Stow it, you 'orrid old crow,' said Benjamin suddenly. 'I'm a proper footman, I am, not that I expects a piece of kennel garbage like yerself to recognize one, not even if you met one in yer soup!'

This was said with such blistering venom that not only Mrs Hick but the whole stage-coach party fell into a deep silence, each one frightened to catch Benjamin's angry eye.

No, thought Hannah, Benjamin had never been a footman before that episode where he had worked for Lady Carsey in Esher, Lady Carsey who had tried to get him hanged for a theft he had not committed, Lady Carsey who liked freaks and wanted Benjamin in her bed. Footmen were indolent creatures and vain. Most would have enjoyed their mistress's discomfiture.

A new waiter bent over Hannah and whispered, 'The gentleman over there, Lord Alistair Munro, wishes the honour of entertaining you.'

Although she was still bewildered and upset by Benjamin, Hannah was glad to escape from the stage-coach passengers.

She rose and went over to Lord Alistair's table. He got up as she approached and drew out a seat for her. Benjamin, with a last threatening look at the cowed passengers, went to stand behind her chair.

'I hope what I have to say will not offend you,' said Lord Alistair. 'I have taken a great liking to your footman. I am sorely tempted to steal him away from you.'

'Wouldn't go,' snapped Benjamin from behind Hannah. 'Not foralla tea 'n China. No.'

'Benjamin,' said Hannah impatiently, 'I am

touched by your loyalty, but you must not address Lord Alistair in such a manner.'

'That's all right,' said Lord Alistair amiably. 'You were very surprised when he spoke.'

Hannah told him the tale of Benjamin's adventures and that led to tales of her other adventures. Lord Alistair appeared fascinated.

'You are a lucky man,' he said to Benjamin at last. 'Many employers would be furious to find that they had been writing reams of instructions to you when all the time you understood every word.'

Benjamin gave a little cough. 'The passengers have left, modom.'

'I did not even notice,' said Hannah, starting up. 'Run and tell them I am just coming.'

Lord Alistair held out his card. 'I am bound for Brighton as well. If I can be of service to you, Mrs . . . ?'

'Pym. *Miss* Pym.'

'Miss Pym. Do not hesitate to call on me.'

Hannah took his card and then hurried out, remembering only when she reached the inn door that she was now the proud possessor of cards of her own, and did not even know yet how Benjamin had come by them.

Benjamin came striding towards her, his face dark with anger. 'The bastards 'as gone,' he shouted.

'I beg your pardon,' said Hannah frostily.

'Sorry, modom, but them passengers must 'ave . . . have . . . told the coachman you was on board and off they've gone, baggage and all.'

Lord Alistair emerged from the inn in time to hear this.

'Well, you are fortunate, Miss Pym,' he said. 'I am just leaving myself and I can take you up. In fact, I can take you all the way to Brighton.'

'Please, my lord,' said Hannah, 'if you could just catch up with the coach so that I may tell them all what I think of them.'

'Gladly.'

Benjamin's eyes lit up as an ostler led a smart curricle up to the front of the inn. The curricle had only recently become fashionable. It was a two-wheeled carriage with a hood and the only two-wheeled carriage which used two horses abreast. It had been damned as ungraceful; the hinder curve of the sword case had been called positively ugly and the crooked front line and the dashing iron in the worst possible taste. But it was the fastest vehicle on the road, being the lightest.

Lord Alistair's was drawn by two matched bays. He helped Hannah in and then climbed in on the other side and took the reins in his hands. Benjamin jumped on the back just as Lord Alistair called to the ostler, 'Stand away.'

To Benjamin's disappointment, the carriage moved off at a leisurely pace.

'I fear, Miss Pym,' said Lord Alistair, 'that being abandoned by the stage-coach is hardly an exciting adventure, merely a tiresome happening.'

'But I have had an adventure,' said Hannah, 'or rather, something terrible has happened.'

'And what was that?'

'Lady Beatrice Marsham was one of the passengers.' Hannah, so eager to share her worries, did not notice a certain rigidity in Lord Alistair's handsome features. 'We stopped at Croydon and we were just about to leave when this ugly-looking individual came up to Lady Beatrice and constrained – I am sure he was holding either a pistol or a knife at her side – constrained her to board his carriage. I cried for help and the coachman and others came running. But when appealed to, Lady Beatrice said she was leaving of her own free will.'

'Did she use those words?' asked Lord Alistair.

'Yes.'

'I'll admit that's odd. It would be more in character for a cold fish like Lady Beatrice Marsham to say, "Damn your impertinence" if all was well.'

'Do you know her?' asked Hannah eagerly.

'I have had that pleasure.' His voice was dry.

'You do not seem to approve of the lady.'

'No, I do not. She plays fast and loose with men's affections, and that was when she was married. Harry Blackstone, her husband that was, died drunk about a year ago. He was gambler, rake and swine in general, but that does not give the lady any excuse to flirt shamelessly until the fellows fall in love with her and then turn them down flat.'

'Were you . . . were you one of those fellows, my lord?'

'No, Miss Pym. I do not pursue married ladies. Change the subject. Lady Beatrice is well able to protect herself. What do you plan to do in Brighton?'

'Look at the sea,' said Hannah with a laugh. 'Walk a great deal. Perhaps I might even see the prince.'

'Bound to see Prinny,' said Lord Alistair. 'Southern's giving a ball next week. Prinny's bound to be there, so you'll see him.'

What an odd day, thought Hannah. First she was humiliated because she thought Lady Beatrice had considered her too low to speak to, and now she was humiliated because Lord Alistair thought her grand enough to be invited to a ball by the Earl of Southern and she would have to explain she was not. 'I am not of the ton,' said Hannah in a stifled voice. 'In fact, I do not really belong anywhere.' In a near whisper, she told him all about her years of service with the Clarences.

He smiled at her. 'Miss Pym, you are a citizen of the world and can go anywhere you like. Tell you what, I'll take you there myself – that is, if you promise to tell me more stories.'

Tears glistened in Hannah's eyes. 'I, my lord? Do you mean that you would take *me*?'

'Yes, Miss Pym. But you'd best tell me where you are staying so that I can call on you.'

'I had not thought,' said Hannah. 'I shall let you know, my lord.'

'Don't know if we'll catch any coach at this rate.' Benjamin's voice sounded from behind them.

'*Really*, Benjamin,' snapped Hannah, wondering if this new Benjamin complete with voice was going to be a problem.

But Lord Alistair smiled lazily and said, 'He has the right of it. Hold tightly. I'm going to spring 'em.'

The horses surged forward and soon Hannah was hanging on for dear life as the now sunny countryside became a moving blur. Behind her, Benjamin, exalted by the speed, began to sing loudly and noisily.

At the bottom of a long hill, they at last saw the coach. On and on they sped. Hannah screamed loudly as they swept past the coach with an inch to spare. Lord Alistair drove his team up the next hill and then swung his carriage around to block the road at the top.

'You was in the coach,' cried the coachman, leaning down from his high perch, his eyes starting from his head as he brought his heavily laden coach to a halt.

'As you can see, I am not,' said Hannah. She climbed down on wobbly legs. 'I am going to continue my journey and I expect a refund on my fare, too. Climb aboard, Benjamin.' But Benjamin had hauled open the door of the coach and had started to berate the passengers.

Hannah pulled him aside and told him to climb on to the roof and then got in to hear the lying protests of the now thoroughly frightened passengers, each protesting that it hadn't been his or her fault. Actually, it had seemed a prime joke to leave Hannah behind when Mrs Hick had suggested it, but now all were scared that Hannah might turn that terrible footman of hers loose on them.

Ignoring them all, Hannah sank back in her seat, only grateful to be secure in the stage-coach once more and resolving never to set foot in another curricle. She hoped the velocity had not damaged her brain.

At last, as night fell, they rolled into Brighton. Hannah was glad, when she booked two rooms at the Ship, that she had managed to force the coaching office to refund some of her fare. The rooms at the Ship were terribly expensive.

Benjamin presented himself in her room.

'Now, Benjamin,' said Hannah sternly, 'out with it. Tell me your story. You may sit down.'

Benjamin sat down on a hard chair opposite and regarded her thoughtfully. 'All of it, modom?' he asked in the stultifying accent he obviously considered genteel.

'Yes, all of it,' said Hannah. 'Start with your parents.'

'I never knew them,' said Benjamin. He told a story of being brought up by a Mrs Coombes in the East End of London in a broken-down house by the river. He could never find out who his parents had been or why Mrs Coombes had taken him in. She drank a lot, he said, and often beat him. He had been apprenticed to a sweep who had got rid of him after only six months because he was growing too big to get up the chimneys. Then he had found work as a stable-lad at a livery stable in the West End. He said he had envied the footmen he saw going about their employers' errands. They seemed to have little to do but dress nicely and look tall. He found he was lucky at gambling and he soon became more interested in that than work. He did not turn up at the livery stable one morning, because he had been up most of the night gambling and had slept in. He lost that job. He felt the

24

loss of it keenly, too, for a clerk who kept the livery stable's books had taught him to read and write. He decided to give up gambling and try to get into service as a footman. But he did not have any references and no one wanted him and he was too tall for a page. He worked as knife-boy in one establishment and then as odd man in another. Then Mrs Coombes, the only sort of family he had ever known, had died. Benjamin had decided to leave London and try to find work as a footman in a country household where they might prove to be less particular than city houses. At Esher, he had learned of Lady Carsey from some men he had gambled with. One of them worked for Lady Carsey as a groom and hinted that she had odd tastes and had once made a pet of a housemaid who had a hunched back. Benjamin hit on the idea of appearing to be deaf and dumb, and for a while it had worked, until Lady Carsey had decided to try to relieve the tedium of her country days by taking the footman into her bed. 'And so you know the rest,' he ended. 'I refused, and she tried to get her revenge.'

Hannah thought uneasily that Benjamin's story was too simple, and yet it could be true. She assured him that she had no intention of turning him off, but added that the inn was too expensive and that they would need to find cheaper lodgings.

'An apartment,' said Benjamin eagerly. 'Then you could make calls an' people could call on you.'

'All very well, Benjamin,' said Hannah, 'but it will be difficult to find someone willing to let us a place for a short time.'

Benjamin struck his breast in a theatrical manner, which was his old way of showing that he would handle the matter, and then gave a shamefaced laugh and said, 'I will find you sump-thin', modom. Leave it to Benjamin.'

'While we are on the subject of calls,' said Hannah, 'where did you manage to get those cards?'

'Printer I used to know,' said Benjamin. 'Did 'em cheap.'

'Then you must tell me what I owe you.'

'Later,' said Benjamin. 'I'll go out now and find us somewhere to live, suitable to our consequences.'

'Consequence,' corrected Hannah, but Benjamin had gone.

He strolled along the seafront, with his hands in his pockets, listening to the waves crashing on the beach, and looking for his prey.

And then he saw three army officers standing by some steps down to the beach. He judged them to be army officers by their whiskers and pigtails rather than by their dress, for none of them was wearing uniform.

He fished in his pocket for his dice, and as he came abreast of them, he dropped the dice to the ground. He bent down and picked them up and said, 'A pair o' sixes.'

One of the officers laughed. 'You couldn't do that again.'

'Try me,' said Benjamin with a grin.

Gambling was a democratic sport. Aristocrats would cheerfully gamble with commoners. They would bet on anything – which goose would cross the road first, which fly would reach the top of the window before the other – and so they all crouched down round Benjamin and started to play hazard dice.

At one point in the game, Benjamin was losing so heavily that he began to think he would have to flee the country, but he persevered and, sure enough, the luck began to run his way.

'Enough,' cried one. 'We have an engagement and we are late already. We will give you our notes of hand.'

'Could suggest something easier for you,' said Benjamin. 'My lady is looking for a snug little apartment for, say, three weeks. Any of you got one? Take that instead of your money.'

The men looked at him in surprise and then one turned to the other and said, 'What say you, Barnstable? Give him the keys to your place and move in with me.'

'Done,' said the one called Barnstable cheerfully.

'Has it got a view of the sea?' asked Benjamin, who thought they were getting off very lightly, for they all owed him a great deal of money.

'I'll take you over,' said Barnstable, 'and give you the keys. Just over there.'

Benjamin followed him to one of the new buildings facing the sea. It turned out to be a pleasant apartment on the ground floor, with a large sitting-room with a bay window that overlooked the sea, a small parlour at the back, then two bedrooms, also at the back, and a kitchen which opened on to a weedy garden.

'My lady will want to move in tomorrow morning,' said Benjamin, looking around. 'Best have your traps moved out tonight. Got a piece o' paper?'

'Why?'

'Want your written agreement.'

'You churl. You little toad. My word is my bond.'

'I've heard that one afore,' said Benjamin. 'You give me that there agreement. My mistress is a Hungarian countess and a friend o' the Prince of Wales.'

'Oh, really?' sneered Barnstable. 'Whoever heard of a countess getting her accommodation this way?'

'Whoever heard o' a countess spending any money she don't have to?'

'Oh, very well.' Barnstable signed an agreement that he would allow Miss Hannah Pym to use his apartment for three weeks. He raised his eyebrows at the name.

'Incognito,' said Benjamin succinctly. 'My lady has a lot of enemies.'

'If this is how she goes about her business, you don't surprise me.'

Benjamin had decided not to tell Hannah about his gambling. Instead he surprised her with a tale about an army man who was only too happy to let her use his place and did not want any payment.

'I find that hard to believe, Benjamin,' commented Hannah suspiciously.

'He was in his cups,' said Benjamin. 'I got him to sign this here agreement, so that when he sobers up, he can't do nuffin' about it.'

Hannah decided to go along with it, and if by chance the mysterious army gentleman had changed his mind, she could always move out again.

2

Mad, bad, and dangerous to know.
Lady Caroline Lamb on Lord Byron

Hannah was delighted with her new residence. She could now look out at the sea all day long if she pleased. But first, the apartment badly needed cleaning. Hannah donned an apron and covered her hair with a mob-cap and set to work until everything was gleaming and shining. As she worked, she thought ruefully that she must do something with Benjamin.

Benjamin appeared to think that a footman's only duties were to stand behind the mistress's chair and carry her letters. Hannah had sent him out two hours ago to deliver a letter to Lord Alistair Munro. She knew he was probably strolling about the streets with his hands in his pockets. It was evident he had learned nothing while he had been in service to Lady Carsey. Probably, while he was in favour, she had made a pet of him.

Her thoughts turned to what she would wear to the ball. She would need to go out that very day and find Brighton's most modish dressmaker and hope that there was some ball gown already made up which had not been collected by the lady who had ordered it.

She picked up two decanters and studied them. They had not been cleaned, so she took them through to the kitchen, filled them with hot water from a kettle swung over the fire, dropped a few pieces of well-soaped brown paper into each, and left them to stand.

She then went back to the sitting-room and opened the windows and leaned out to smell the fresh salt tang of the sea.

Benjamin came strolling along, whistling, hands in his pockets, and turned in at the gate.

Hannah shook her head in disapproval. A footman should always look as if he were on duty, whether his mistress was with him or not.

So when Benjamin appeared in the sitting-room, Hannah asked him sharply if he would like to learn to be a 'real' footman.

'I thought I was, modom,' said Benjamin, very stiffly on his stiffs.

Hannah shook her head. 'You are a good lad, but you must learn that there is more to being a footman than parading about in livery. What would become of you if I were to die? Now, would you like to be properly trained?'

Benjamin nodded eagerly.

But the look of eagerness left his face as Hannah went on ... and on ... and on.

A footman should never hand over anything at all without putting it on a tray first, and always hand it with the left hand and on the left side of the person he serves, and hold it so the guest may take it with ease. In lifting dishes from the table, he should use both hands. This was because, as one foreign visitor to England had noted, 'A complete English repast suggested the reason why such large English dishes are to be seen in silver, pewter, china, and crockery shops; to wit, because a quarter of a calf, half a lamb, and monstrous pieces of meat are dished up, and everyone receives almost an entire fish.'

After each meal, the footman's place is at the sink. He should have one wooden bowl of hot water for washing dishes, and one wooden bowl for rinsing. There was less chance of breakages if wood was used. He should rub down the furniture in the sitting-room and parlour before breakfast and then be washed and clean and neat, prepared to go out with his mistress.

He should mind his own business at all times. 'There was once a footman at Thornton Hall,' said Hannah, 'who would stand behind Mrs Clarence's chair and advise her how to play her cards. You must never do anything like that, Benjamin. I had to speak to that footman very sharply. Also, what your mistress says at the table is none of your business. If a guest is telling a very funny story, you must not even dare to laugh. A good footman should be quiet, almost invisible. You have hitherto been saved all household chores, for I have been in the way of looking after myself. Now, I have put two decanters to soak. This afternoon, empty them out, fill them up with clean water, and add a little muriatic acid, and then leave them to stand. It is very hard to clean dirty decanters.

'I have cleaned here very thoroughly, so you may be excused from proper duties today. But remember, some footmen have a very hard time. Gentlemen often take their footmen with them when they go out of an evening, for the footman's duty is to pick his master up from under the table where said master has fallen after a bout of heavy drinking. If the footman does not remove the master quietly and gracefully from the room, he may lose his job, for if his friends mock him the next day for his drunkenness, he will not blame himself but his footman for not having saved him from ridicule. It is not an easy life.'

Benjamin looked crestfallen for a moment, but then brightened. 'I will do as well as I can for you, modom,' he said, 'but, saints preserve us, if you was ever to go to your Maker, I certainly wouldn't work for one of those gents what you was talking about.'

'Then decide what you *do* want to do,' retorted Hannah tartly. 'For if a life in service don't suit, then you'd better start thinking about apprenticing yourself to some trade. Now, we shall go out. I must find a dressmaker and hope she or he has a made-up gown for sale, for I am determined to go to that ball!'

Hannah, by dint of visiting the circulating library, found out from the gentleman in charge of it that the main dressmaker of Brighton was Monsieur Blanc. Monsieur Blanc was a voluble man with a strong French accent. He said in answer to Hannah's request that he had not only one, but three ball gowns which had not been collected. One of them, to Hannah's delight, was perfect. It was a heavy white satin slip with a rich overdress of gold satin fastened down the front with gold clasps. It could have been made for her. She tried it on and hardly recognized Hannah Pym in the elegant creature that looked back at her from the glass.

'A mere eight hundred guineas,' cooed Monsieur Blanc.

'Cor!' said Benjamin in awe.

Hannah turned a little pale.

'I have not yet made up my mind,' she said. 'I should like to take a little walk and think about it.'

Monsieur Blanc looked disappointed but, ever hopeful, said he was sure that, after a little thought, she would realize the folly of turning down such an exquisite creation.

With Benjamin a few paces behind her, she walked sadly down one of Brighton's twisting, cobbled streets. 'Eight hundred guineas,' said Hannah over her shoulder. 'It's wicked, that's what it is. Wicked! I should be ruined if I paid that.'

'Beg parding,' said Benjamin. 'I left my gloves in that Frog's shop.'

'The fact that we are at war with the French does

not mean you can go about calling respectable French tradesmen Frogs,' snapped Hannah. 'Oh, go for your gloves. I shall be in that pastry cook's shop over there.'

Benjamin ran off. He opened the door of the dressmaker's and went inside. 'Has your mistress decided?' asked Monsieur Blanc.

'Fact is,' said Benjamin, 'my lady is strapped for the readies. O' course, she could ask 'er friend, the Prince o' Wales, but these foreign royalties is very proud. Very.'

Monsieur Blanc looked bewildered. 'But she introduced herself as a visitor to Brighton called Miss Pym.'

Benjamin grinned and tapped the side of his nose. 'Incognito,' he said. 'Don't want it spread about and I know a man in your position has to be discreet, but you know how it's got around that Mrs Fitzherbert's had her day.'

'Bless me,' said the dressmaker in accents almost as Cockney as Benjamin's. 'He married her, didn't he?'

'Mrs Fitzherbert ... garn,' said Benjamin, now more confident because Monsieur Blanc had revealed himself to be not French but very English, and East End of London English at that. 'The marriage can't be reckernized. You knows that and I knows that. Our prince is getting tired o' her, like I said. An' why's he tired o' her? 'Cos my mistress has caught his eye.'

Everyone knew the prince's penchant for ladies older than himself. Even so, Monsieur Blanc looked bewildered. 'But what has it got to do with me?'

'Well, see 'ere. This Miss Pym – we'll call her that, hey? – she's going to Lord Southern's ball. If you were to lend her that gown for a night, then she could tell all it was you she got it from and that she wouldn't dream o' getting her gowns and pretties from anyone else. Of course, the prince himself would get to hear of it.'

'My stars and garters.' Monsieur Blanc clasped his hands.

'But you're not to tell a soul who she really is. Promise.'

'I don't know who she really is!'

'But you know now she's a foreign princess what has taken the prince's eye. So promise.'

'Promise, as sure as my name's Blanc.'

'Which it ain't,' said Benjamin with a cheeky grin.

Monsieur Blanc grinned back. 'You're a sharp one. It's White, so it's the same thing really, blanc being the French for white. Don't you go letting out I'm not French – the ladies liking to think they got a Frenchie to make their dresses – and I'll let you have the gown. You can take it now. But tell Miss Pym she's got to tell His Highness about me.'

'Would I lie?' Benjamin sat down in a little gilt chair and folded his arms. 'If you box it up, I'll take it to her.'

Hannah wondered what had become of him and whether he might have lost his way. She was just about to leave the pastry cook's and go in search of him when he came running in, carrying a large box.

'The dress, modom,' he whispered.

'Oh, heavens!' wailed Hannah. 'You've stolen it.'

'That's a right fine thing to say to your trusted servant!' exclaimed Benjamin. 'I went back to the shop and he ups and says you can borrow it for the evening; only, if anyone compliments you on it, you're to say you gets all your gowns offa him. Right?'

'Well, of course I'll do that,' said Hannah. 'Are you sure?'

'O' course,' said Benjamin loftily. 'It's the way he goes about advertising. They all do that. Bless my heart, modom, but you are as innocent as a new-born lamb. Them grand ladies, why, a lot of them haven't paid for a stitch that's on their backs.'

This was almost true, as a great number paid their dressmaking bills only when faced with the threat of duns, and some did not pay at all.

'Why, Benjamin, you are amazing. You may sit down with me and take tea.'

'Won't do,' said Benjamin sternly. 'You have to know what's due to your position. I'll get some newspapers and we'll take that box 'ome . . . home . . . and I'll have me tea there.'

They bought newspapers and groceries, Hannah disappointed to find the prices were as high as in London. They returned to their temporary home and Hannah said that Benjamin could take the newspapers through to the parlour while she prepared dinner. She went to the kitchen and made up the fire and put a joint of roast iamb on the spit. Benjamin appeared in the kitchen, holding a newspaper. 'What was the name of the frosty-faced female what was on the coach?'

'That,' said Hannah repressively, 'was Lady Beatrice Marsham.'

'She's in the newspapers. Her engagement's written right 'ere.'

'To whom?'

'Sir Geoffrey Handford.'

Hannah shook her head in amazement. 'To think of all the fuss I made! She must have thought me quite mad.'

'It also says she's here in Brighton, staying with Mrs Handford, Sir Geoffrey's ma.'

'Worse and worse,' moaned Hannah, shaking her head at her own folly. 'And there I was crying out that she was being taken away by force. I must say, this news does relieve my conscience, for when Lord Alistair told me that Lady Beatrice was well able to take care of herself, I believed him, but last night I found myself worrying about her again.'

'You can call on her anyway,' said Benjamin. 'I mean, she gave you her card. Got to meet a few of the nobs, ha'nt you?'

'Well, yes, I could call. Can you find Mrs Handford's address?'

'Easy,' said Benjamin.

He was back in about ten minutes. 'Mrs Handford's just around hard by. One of those big houses on the Steyne.'

'How did you find out so quickly?'

'Thought it might be one of them grand houses, so I asked any servant I saw about and got it the third time of asking.'

'I wonder if I should go,' mused Hannah. 'I mean, I would be social climbing, would I not? And what if I were damned as a mushroom?'

'Well, if that's yer attitude, you'd best kiss that Sir George Clarence good-bye.'

'Benjamin! I allow you a good deal of licence, but I would not have allowed a footman to address me in such terms even were I still only a housekeeper.'

'Sorry, modom,' said Benjamin stiffly.

Hannah looked at him for a few moments and then said reluctantly, 'Oh, very well.'

Late that afternoon, Monsieur Blanc called at the household of a certain Mrs Cambridge. Mrs Cambridge was very elegant, a member of the untitled aristocracy and one of Monsieur Blanc's best customers. With a mouthful of pins, he carefully arranged a seam and said, 'T' shtrangesht shing 'appened today.'

'What?' demanded Mrs Cambridge, twisting round. 'Do take those pins out of your mouth. It is hard to understand you at the best of times.'

Monsieur Blanc complied. 'Zee strangest thing 'appened this day,' he said, his accent stronger than ever, for he regretted bitterly having let it slip in front of Benjamin. 'Zis lady, ver' grand, came into my salon. She is amazed at my work. She says she will buy everything from me. She call 'erself Miss Pym. 'Er footman, he return to collect the gown I 'ave fashioned for 'er, and he tells me,' went on Monsieur Blanc, dropping most of his accent suddenly in his desire to impart such a stunning piece of gossip, 'that this Miss Pym, is, in fact, foreign royalty. Oh, *ma foi!* Why did I tell you? It is so secret.'

'Really!' Mrs Cambridge's eyes glowed. 'You silly man. You know I won't tell a soul.'

'My lips are sealed.'

'Such a pity. I was going to order a whole new summer wardrobe from you.'

'But it eez gossip of the most dangerous.'

'Pity about that wardrobe. I meant to have at least a dozen ensembles.'

Like the shrewd man he was, Monsieur Blanc guessed that the bidding had now gone as high as he could expect it to go. Twelve ensembles was top offer. With affected reluctance, he said, 'I must remember that Madame is so discreet.'

'Exactly.'

'Well,' whispered Monsieur Blanc, 'her footman told me that our Prince of Wales is madly in love with this Miss Pym, or so she chooses to call herself.'

Mrs Cambridge looked at him with her mouth open. Never since the Prince of Wales had become betrothed to Mrs Fitzherbert had such a delicious piece of scandal come to Brighton. 'I will not breathe a word,' she said.

'And so,' said Mrs Cambridge to a rapt audience of ladies over the tea-tray that evening, 'what do you think of *that*?'

'Where does she live?' asked a faded little blonde.

'In an apartment on the front promenade. Number two.'

'We must leave cards,' said another.

'You had best let me go first,' said Mrs Cambridge. 'May be all a hum.'

Hannah was just dressing to go out the following day when Benjamin announced there was a Mrs Cambridge to see her.

Puzzled, Hannah told Benjamin to put the visitor in the drawing-room and tell her that she would be with her directly. Hannah finished dressing and then walked through to the drawing-room.

In a rustle of silks and a fluttering of feathers, Mrs Cambridge swept Hannah a court curtsy. Taken aback, Hannah returned the salute with a startled nod, rather like a shying horse.

'I heard you had honoured our little resort with your presence, Miss ... er ... Pym.'

'And who told you, ma'am?' asked Hannah, waving a hand to indicate that Mrs Cambridge should sit down. 'Lord Alistair Munro?'

'No, no. Another person. But I am bound to secrecy. How do you like our watering-place?'

'It is very beautiful,' said Hannah, looking bewildered.

'And what do you think of our most famous resident, the Prince of Wales?'

Hannah was a royalist to the tip of her fingers. She had never seen the prince but had seen some very flattering prints and engravings of him. 'His Highness is a model of what all gentlemen should be,' she said firmly. 'Such handsome looks, such a regal bearing, such exquisite taste.'

'Exactly what we all think of him,' breathed Mrs Cambridge.

She stared at Hannah as if memorizing every detail.

Hannah shifted uncomfortably. 'As it happens, Mrs Cambridge, I was just on the point of going out. I am paying a call on Lady Beatrice Marsham.'

Mrs Cambridge shot to her feet. 'I shall not keep you. Shall we have the honour of your presence at Lord Southern's ball?'

'Yes, I shall be there.'

'Splendid. May I presume to hope that we may become friends?'

Hannah was more bewildered than ever. 'You may,' she said. 'And now I really must go.'

'I shall not detain you any longer,' said Mrs Cambridge and, to Hannah's amazement, she rose and dropped another court curtsy and then *backed* from the room.

'Well!' exclaimed Hannah when she had gone. 'Tell me, Benjamin, am I so far out of the world that I do not know how folks go on? I thought one only retreated like that before royalty.'

'It's the sea air, modom,' said Benjamin, ignoring a stab of guilt, for he was sure the dressmaker had blabbed about Hannah being foreign royalty. 'It addles people's brains, or so I have read.'

'*And*,' said Mrs Cambridge a bare quarter of an hour later to her friends, who had been waiting in her drawing-room for her return from the call, 'when I curtsied, she only replied with a common nod, just the way royalty goes on, you know. And her voice is so un-English, very clear and every word carefully enounced. And her regal bearing softened when she spoke of the prince. If only you could have seen and heard her.'

'What does she look like?' asked one.

Mrs Cambridge settled down to give a thorough description, and as she talked, Hannah's crooked nose was straightened, her spare housekeeper's figure showed all the signs of royal birth, her sandy hair grew brown, and her sallow skin 'white as alabaster'. 'And,' went on Mrs Cambridge, 'she was just leaving to call on Lady Beatrice Marsham. When did Lady Beatrice ever trouble to receive any lady? Mark my words, Lady Beatrice would only stoop to receive royalty. So there!'

'Miss Pym,' said Mrs Handford's butler, 'to see Lady Beatrice.'

Mrs Handford sat next to Lady Beatrice on a backless sofa in her drawing-room. She was a squat, powerful, pugnacious woman who looked remarkably like a bulldog guarding a juicy bone.

'Lady Beatrice is not at home,' said Mrs Handford.

Lady Beatrice held up her hand. 'You had best allow this lady to come up,' she said coldly. 'Miss Pym raised a great commotion at the inn when your son abducted me. If she does not find me apparently safe and well, she may make a fuss.'

'Geoffrey told me about some spinster yelling and fussing. Very well. Have her up, but remember what will happen to you if you make her suspicious.'

'I know what will happen to me. My dear parents have told me that they will cut me off without a shilling if I do not marry Geoffrey. Geoffrey and you have hinted at dark things. You need have no fear. If you all wish to see me wed to another man whom I detest, that is your affair.'

Hannah came in and smiled tentatively at Lady Beatrice. Lady Beatrice rose gracefully, introduced her to Mrs Handford, and asked Hannah to sit down. She then sank down on the sofa beside Mrs Handford and said colourlessly, 'How kind of you to call. How did you know my direction? It was not on the card I gave you.'

'It was in the newspapers along with your engagement. May I offer my felicitations?'

Lady Beatrice nodded briefly. There was a long silence.

'Staying long?' barked Mrs Handford suddenly.

'A few weeks,' said Hannah, her eyes still on Lady Beatrice, who was sitting as still as a statue. 'I have found pleasant lodgings where I can see the sea from my drawing-room. If your ladyship would care to call . . . ?'

'Too busy,' snapped Mrs Handford. 'Getting married soon.'

Hannah did not like it. She did not like it at all. There was a thin air of veiled menace emanating from the ugly Mrs Handford, and Lady Beatrice was so

44

white and still. All her fears for Lady Beatrice came rushing back.

Hannah began to chatter about the weather, about the beneficial effects of sea air, about the fashionable crowd which thronged Brighton's streets.

'You should try sea bathing, Miss Pym,' said Lady Beatrice.

'I do not know how to swim,' exclaimed Hannah.

'That is not necessary. You get a bathing machine to take you out and the lady in charge will make sure you do not drown.'

'Oh, I would like to try that,' said Hannah, her eyes shining, and was relieved to see Lady Beatrice smile.

'If you will excuse us,' said Mrs Handford rudely, 'we were just about to discuss the wedding arrangements.'

Hannah rose and took her leave.

Once outside, she confided her fears to Benjamin. 'Rum go,' said the footman. 'Let's go call on that Lord Alistair. He'll know what to do.'

Lord Alistair was at home and pleased to receive Miss Pym. She asked him shyly if he still meant to take her to the ball and flushed with happiness when he said he did.

'I have just been to call on Lady Beatrice,' said Hannah.

'She does have an odd taste in husbands, that lady,' commented Lord Alistair drily. 'I see she is engaged to Sir Geoffrey Handford. Handford is a bully and a brute.'

'I did not meet him, but I met Mrs Handford,' said Hannah. 'She made me feel uneasy. Bless me, but I had this odd impression that she was *guarding* Lady Beatrice.'

'I do not think for a moment there is anything amiss,' said Lord Alistair easily. 'Think on the character of Lady Beatrice. She is not a sweet virgin to be easily bullied. She is a widow in her late twenties. She is cold and hard and assured. She can drive better than most men. Her late husband, Blackstone, was, I admit, a degenerate fiend and would have broken the spirit of a meeker woman.'

'Why did she marry this Blackstone?'

'Her parents, the Earl and Countess of Debren, arranged it. Medieval couple. Give me the shudders. Live in a great moated castle in Warwickshire. The countess gave birth to Beatrice when she was in her forties and reputed to be long past child-bearing. Why Blackstone? That's simple. He was the one prepared to pay the most to marry her. I saw her at her first Season. Different creature entirely, sweet and shy. Anyway, the earl and countess, not content with the marriage settlement, hoped to get their hands on some of the Blackstone fortune. But Harry Blackstone used to gamble thousands and thousands of guineas a night. I believe he left nothing but debts on his death. Now Geoffrey Handford is a rich nabob, made his killing in India. That's the attraction. If Lady Beatrice doesn't like Sir Geoffrey, that would be a pity were she a pleasant female. Friend of mine, Captain Jarret, became obsessed with her. She flirted with him quite shamelessly. Blackstone was never around to stop the flirtation, for he was always in the card-room or dead drunk. The captain asked her to run away with him, and she suddenly turned as cold as ice and told him haughtily that he was over-stepping the mark. Broke his heart.'

'Hearts do not break, Lord Alistair,' said Hannah. 'Your friend was at fault for chasing after a married lady.'

'You haven't seen Lady Beatrice in action, Miss Pym. Quite dazzling. Gives a fellow a smile that promises him the world and more. Lady Beatrice is not worth your concern. Tell me instead about yourself.'

They passed a pleasant half-hour and Hannah finally left, feeling sure that, after all, she had been silly to pity or worry about Lady Beatrice.

When she returned home, she was startled to see a group of people at her gate. As she passed, the men raised their hats and the women curtsied.

'What was that about?' asked Hannah faintly when they were safely indoors.

'Very simple people in these seaside places,' said Benjamin quickly. 'Like to pay their courtesies to a new face in town.'

'How very odd,' said Hannah Pym.

'So that's her,' said Sir Geoffrey Handford to his friend, Mr Gully Parks. 'Old fright, ain't she? What did you say her name was?'

'Pym. Miss Hannah Pym, or rather, that's what she's calling herself.'

'And Prinny is spoony about that crooked-nosed bat?'

'On the best authority, old chap. On the v-e-r-y best authority. You want to be Lord Thingummy, that's your road. Butter her up and get her to pop a word in the royal ear.'

3

*Vaulting ambition, which o'erleaps itself
And falls on the other.*

William Shakespeare

Sir Geoffrey made his way home deep in thought. His ambition was to have a title – baron, viscount, earl or marquis. To this end, he had been cultivating friends of the Prince of Wales, and sending the prince handsome presents. So far, all he had received for his pains had been a slight nod from the prince at a ball.

He wandered into his mother's drawing-room, still trying to work out a way to introduce himself to this Miss Pym.

'I am glad you are home, Geoffrey,' said his mother. 'I've had a tiresome afternoon.'

'Beatrice coming over nasty again?'

'No, but cold and insolent as usual. She had a visitor.'

Sir Geoffrey's face darkened. 'She isn't supposed to have any visitors. Where is she?'

'Gone to sulk in her room.'

'And why did you allow this visitor to see her?'

'It was that female you told me about, you know, the one who set up the row at the inn. I handled her. Lady Beatrice knows what she's supposed to do. Not by a flicker did she show that anything was amiss.'

'What's the name of this interfering busybody anyway?'

'Miss Hannah Pym.'

Sir Geoffrey sat down suddenly. 'Is she a middle-aged woman with a bent nose?'

'Yes. You should know. You saw her at the inn.'

'I didn't pay her any heed. I was too concerned with getting Beatrice away. Let me tell you, sainted Mother, that this Miss Pym is not what she seems. Travelling by stage-coach must have been an effort on her part to arrive quietly in Brighton. It is said that she is Prinny's latest amour: and not only that – of foreign royalty.'

'Tish, and fiddlesticks. Who is spreading such rubbish?'

'Letitia Cambridge.'

'Mrs Cambridge. Good heavens above!'

'Exactly.'

Mrs Cambridge was accounted among the cream of the ton.

'Furthermore, Mrs Cambridge called on this Miss

Pym, not really believing a word of the gossip, but came away perfectly convinced it was true. And you know how that bitch is too easy to damn people as parvenus and upstarts,' said Sir Geoffrey with feeling, he and his mother having been at the receiving end of Mrs Cambridge's high-handedness. 'This could be the entrée I need. I've done everything I can to try to get Prinny's ear, and nothing has worked.'

'She asked Beatrice to call on her,' said Mrs Handford.

'Then Beatrice had better go. The sooner she forges a friendship with this Miss Pym, or whoever she is, the better.'

'And then what? Beatrice will promptly tell her all about the marriage she is being forced into.'

'No, I do not think she will. Her parents have already told her through me that if she does not wed me, they will cut her off without a shilling. There is nothing else she can do but obey me. In fact, I think we should risk turning her loose. She can go to that house she has rented and do what she likes. She cannot escape me – that is, unless she wishes to end up a pauper.'

Mrs Handford shifted her large bulk uneasily. 'Do you really think her parents would go ahead and do such a thing?'

'Oh, yes; they said they had brought her to heel over that marriage to Blackstone in the same way.'

'But she was, what? Eighteen when she married him. She's a hardened widow of twenty-eight now. Oh, I wish you had not been so dramatic, Geoffrey.

51

There was no need to force her into your carriage at gunpoint. Would it not be better to promise her her freedom if she does all in her power to use her influence with Miss Pym? Surely a title means more to you than a chilly widow who hates you.'

'No, Mama. I want her and that's that. I admit I should not have chased her down the Brighton road, but I was mad with fury when I heard she had left London. I did not know then that her parents were going to do all in their power to force the marriage through. I did not get their letter until I arrived here. Let her go. She'll accept this marriage with good grace, you'll see.'

'And what if some other man snatches her up in the meantime?'

'No man will. Not now. Not with her reputation. She's broken so many hearts that it's become almost a point of honour *not* to even be seen dancing with her. She was at Derby's ball two weeks ago and spent most of the evening with the wallflowers. A sad come-down for London's beauty, who used to have 'em fighting over her on the ballroom floor. That's why I'm confident she'll end up looking forward to this marriage. I'm a handsome fellow.'

'You are that,' said his mother, gazing at him with affection. In that moment, both looked remarkably alike with their bulldog faces and long wide mouths that seemed to stretch from ear to ear.

'Right! Fetch her in here and I'll tell her what she's got to do.'

A footman was summoned and told to fetch Lady

Beatrice. 'Make yourself scarce, Mama,' said Sir Geoffrey. 'May as well kick off with a little wooing.'

Lady Beatrice hesitated on the threshold when she saw that he was alone.

'What is it?' she demanded.

He looked at her, at her elegant figure and the beauty of her face, and his senses quickened. She would be magnificent as his wife. He looked forward to getting her in his bed. He was sure there were a few interesting tricks he could show her. That drunk, Blackstone, couldn't have been much of a lover.

'Come sit by me, my sweeting,' he said.

Lady Beatrice took a few steps into the room. 'I would rather stay here,' she said, 'in case you decide to hold a gun on me again.'

'You must forgive me,' he said, putting his hand on his heart. 'I would not hurt you for the world.'

'Then release me from this engagement.'

'Always funning, ain't you? How would you like to move to your own place?'

Lady Beatrice looked startled. 'With all my heart.'

'Well, and so you may. This very day, in fact. There is something I want you to do for me.'

'That being?'

'You know that Miss Pym?'

'Of course.'

'Did you know she was Prinny's latest flirt?'

Lady Beatrice began to laugh. 'Prinny's . . . ? You must be mad. She is a respectable English lady and, I believe, every bit the spinster she claims to be.'

'Letitia Cambridge says she is of foreign royalty and

Prinny dotes on her, and I want you to call on her and get her to put a word in Prinny's ear about getting me a lordship or an earldom.'

Lady Beatrice opened her mouth to say that Mrs Cambridge was, and always had been, a silly gossip. But then she quickly realized that her freedom, or temporary freedom, from the terrible Handfords somehow depended on her cultivating a friendship with Miss Pym.

She affected surprise. 'Well, I never would have believed such a thing. Now you come to mention it, she did have a certain regal bearing and I was most surprised to find her travelling on the stage.'

'Probably hoped to slip quietly into Brighton. Will you do it?'

'Yes, if you will let me leave this evening.'

'And you will promise not to tell her about *your* parents' forcing you to accept me? For, you know, I have only to break off the engagement and tell them it was all your fault for them to turn you out in the street.'

'I will do what you wish,' said Lady Beatrice. 'Tell me, Sir Geoffrey, why on earth do you want to marry me?'

'Come here and I'll show you.' He leered at her and she backed away, repulsed.

'I will call on Miss Pym tomorrow,' said Lady Beatrice quickly. 'But you cannot expect me to ask her any favours right away. I must, you will agree, forge some sort of friendship. The whole of Brighton will be trying to cultivate her society.'

'Don't be too long about it,' he said.

Lady Beatrice turned and left the room. She almost ran to her bedchamber and then rang for the maid and told her that her bags were to be packed and delivered to her house in Brighton. Then, swinging a cloak about her shoulders, she went downstairs.

The butler loomed up just as she was making for the door.

'I am afraid the master has not given you permission to leave, my lady,' he said.

'That's all right, Foskins,' said Sir Geoffrey's voice from the stairs. 'Lady Beatrice may go.'

Lady Beatrice looked up at him, at his thick gross body and heavy face, and then turned quickly away. The butler held open the door and she walked out, trying hard not to run. After she had gone a little way away, she stood and breathed in great gulps of fresh, salty air.

Hannah was becoming alarmed. The following day, there were so many people clustered outside her flat that she was frightened to go out.

By the afternoon, Benjamin was kept busy turning away visitors, saying that Miss Pym was 'not at home'.

'There is something badly wrong here,' said Hannah. 'I cannot look out at the sea, for when I try to, I find myself staring into the eyes of so many watchers. Enough is enough, and you are looking shiftier and guiltier by the minute. There is no reason for so many people to try to call, now is there? Out with it, Benjamin. I shall find out sooner or later, you know.'

'You promise not to turn me off?' said Benjamin desperately.

'Oh, very well, for I would do anything now to get at the truth.'

'Modom, I did it to get you that ball gown. I told Monsieur Blanc that you was a foreign princess . . .'

'Heavens!'

'There's worse.' Benjamin's head sank lower. 'I told him that you were the Prince of Wales's latest fancy.'

'WHAT? Benjamin, this will reach the ears of the prince and we shall both be in the Tower. Oh, you silly fool. What am I to do? I cannot go to that ball now. And you must take that gown back immediately and tell Monsieur Blanc that you were lying. And tell anyone else who will listen.'

'They won't believe me,' said Benjamin gloomily. 'You're supposed to be incognito, so they'll think you've instructed me to lie to everyone. You see, they would rather believe the lie.'

Hannah began to pace up and down the back parlour. 'I need help,' she said. 'This is appalling. Oh, there's the knocker again. Send whoever it is away.'

Benjamin opened the door to Lady Beatrice. He recognized her immediately. 'I am afraid Miss Pym is not at home, my lady,' he said.

Lady Beatrice calmly walked past him and then into the drawing-room. Benjamin slammed the door on the watching crowd and followed her.

She was standing by the fireplace, drawing off her gloves. 'I will wait,' she said.

Benjamin was about to say that Miss Pym was not

expected back till midnight when the lady herself walked into the room.

'It is all right, Benjamin,' said Hannah quietly. 'You may leave us. Pray be seated, Lady Beatrice. Before you begin to speak, I must tell you that I am not of royal blood, nor have I ever met the Prince of Wales.'

'I suspected as much,' said Lady Beatrice with a little sigh.

'I wish I had never come to Brighton,' said Hannah passionately. 'First, on the road down, I had a mad idea that you were being abducted, and now, because of my footman, lies about me are circulating all around Brighton and I dare not show my face out of doors.'

'Why did your footman start such rumours?' asked Lady Beatrice.

'I do not want to tell you for reasons of pride.' Hannah blinked away the tears that had come to her eyes. 'Oh, I may as well tell you all. I will never see you again, but it will give me some relief to unburden myself. I am plain common Miss Hannah Pym, formerly housekeeper to the late Mr Clarence of Thornton Hall, Kensington. He left me a legacy and so I found myself a lady of independent means. After you had left the coach, I met by chance Lord Alistair Munro. The coach went off and left me behind and Lord Alistair took me in his carriage so that I might catch up on the coach. And so we did. But on the journey, Lord Alistair graciously offered to take me to Lord Southern's ball, and Lord Alistair knows exactly who I am. I was elated. I went to Monsieur Blanc, the dressmaker, to see if he had a gown already made up, which he had, and it was a perfect fit.

'Alas, the price was eight hundred guineas, almost a fifth of my small inheritance. I refused. My footman went back, saying he had left his gloves, and spun the dressmaker a parcel of lies about me being of foreign royalty and that I was the Prince of Wales's latest amour.'

Lady Beatrice felt like laughing. She realized in the same moment she had not felt like laughing until she had met Hannah Pym.

'But I was under the impression your footman was deaf and dumb?'

'Oh, I wish he were!' cried Hannah. 'But that is another story and so very long. You may take your leave now, Lady Beatrice, and if you have a spark of compassion in you, you will tell as many people as possible that I am a fraud.'

'I do not think they would believe me,' said Lady Beatrice. 'You *are* supposed to be incognito, you know.'

'Then I shall leave Brighton this very evening!'

'And not go to the ball? Miss Pym, you have been very frank with me, and so I must be frank with you. You did not imagine I was being abducted.'

To the amazed Hannah she told of her forced engagement and her parents' threat and how she had only secured her brief freedom from Sir Geoffrey and his mother by promising to try to get Miss Pym to use her influence on Sir Geoffrey's behalf to get him a title.

It was no use, Hannah reflected, to protest that parents did not force their daughters into marriage, when there was ample proof of it almost every day. Marriages were mostly business deals, and money was at the root of all such arrangements.

'And you have no money of your own?' asked Hannah.

'No. My husband gambled away a vast fortune and left me debts. My parents paid those debts and settled a generous allowance on me. I naïvely thought my worries were over.'

'But have you no aunts, uncles, other relations to appeal to for help?'

'My parents are elderly now: my aunts and uncles are dead. I have two nephews, both in India, that is all.'

Hannah twisted her fingers in distress. 'My dear Lady Beatrice, if I thought I could get away with this masquerade which has been thrust upon me, I would for your sake. For when you tell Sir Geoffrey that it is not true – and *he* is bound to believe you, knowing that you have every reason to hope it to be true – then you will be forced to return to his mother's house.'

'Perhaps not,' said Lady Beatrice. 'He was not so sure of me until my parents' letter reached him after we had arrived in Brighton. In it, they assured him that they would turn me out into the street if I did not wed him. But as to your problem, I do not have the ear of the Prince of Wales, but Lord Alistair Munro does. I do not know him very well, but I know he is much admired. Why not send for him and tell him all?'

Hannah looked at her with hope dawning on her face. 'Will he not think me ridiculous?'

'I shall be amazed if he does. Most of society, on the other hand, is ridiculous. He has probably heard the gossip already.'

Hannah went to a desk in the corner and pulled forward a sheet of paper. 'I shall send Benjamin with a note. Oh, how I wish you could stay, for I dread to think what he will say.'

'I will stay,' said Lady Beatrice. 'No doubt Sir Geoffrey has one of his servants stationed outside this house to report how I am faring. When he hears that I spent a long time with you, he will be in alt. I have no intention of disabusing him. Let him find out for himself.'

Benjamin was sent with the note and Hannah went through to the kitchen to make tea, happy that as Lady Beatrice knew her circumstances, she did not have to pretend to have a host of servants tucked away. She clucked angrily when she saw that the twenty-two-pound sugar loaf which Benjamin had brought in that morning was still sitting there, looking as hard as granite. She then reflected that Benjamin had not been trained and therefore did not yet know his duties, and she chipped off the required amount, pounded it into granules, and put it into a sugar-bowl.

When she went back into the parlour, she found that Lady Beatrice had fallen silently and soundlessly asleep in her chair. Hannah set down the tray of tea-things on a table, wondering whether to wake her, wondering why the chilly Lady Beatrice had elected to stay. She did not look hard or cold in sleep, but young and vulnerable.

A log fell on the hearth and Lady Beatrice awoke instantly and blinked and looked around.

'I am sorry, Miss Pym,' she said, 'but I have not slept well since I arrived in Brighton.'

Hannah poured tea. 'I must warn you, Lady Beatrice,' she said awkwardly, 'that although Lord Alistair has been extremely kind to me, he does not appear to approve of you.'

'How so? I barely know the man.'

Hannah hesitated.

'Out with it. We have both been so frank with each other, 'twere a pity to dissemble now.'

'Lord Alistair, I regret to say, damns you as a heartless flirt.'

'What ails the man? We all flirt. 'Tis the fashion.'

'He had a friend, a captain, and he said you encouraged his advances, only to break his heart.'

'Fustian.' Lady Beatrice coloured and turned her head slightly away.

Hannah heard a key turning in the front door. 'That is Benjamin,' she said. 'Let us hope he brought Lord Alistair with him.'

Lord Alistair strolled into the parlour and put up his quizzing-glass and stared for a few moments at Lady Beatrice. Then he turned to Hannah. 'You wished to see me, Miss Pym?'

'Yes, please, my lord. I am in the most dreadful difficulties. But pray be seated and have some tea.'

Lord Alistair sat down in an armchair and crossed his booted legs. His golden hair gleamed in the firelight, but his blue eyes were alert and watchful and Hannah knew that he did not like the presence of Lady Beatrice.

But she needed help and so she told the whole story of Benjamin's deception. Lord Alistair carefully placed his cup on the table and leaned back in his chair and laughed and laughed.

'It is no laughing matter,' said Hannah distractedly. 'What am I to do?'

Lord Alistair wiped his eyes and then grinned at Hannah. 'I think your main worry is that the prince himself should get to hear of it and send someone over from the Pavilion to read you a lecture. I shall call on Prinny and hope your story amuses him as much as it has amused me.'

'I wanted Lady Beatrice to go around telling everyone that it is all untrue, but she said she would not be believed.'

'But I will be,' said Lord Alistair, 'for everyone knows I am a confidant of the prince. Your worries will soon be over, Miss Pym. By tomorrow, there will be no one at your gate.'

'Thank you, my lord,' said Hannah, and then turned red.

'There is something else?'

'It all started with that gown. It will need to be taken back. I do not have a ball gown.'

'That is no problem,' said Lady Beatrice. 'We are of the same size in height and both slim. I will send my maid round with something suitable which she can alter to fit you.'

Lord Alistair gazed at Lady Beatrice in surprise. 'You amaze me, madam,' he said. 'I thought you cared for neither man, woman, or beast.'

'You do not know me,' retorted Lady Beatrice haughtily.

'Evidently not.' Lord Alistair rose to his feet. 'Miss Pym, the ball is on Wednesday. I shall call for you at eight.' He bowed and left.

The Prince of Wales was studying plans that would turn his Marine Pavilion into an oriental palace. When he was told that Lord Alistair Munro was demanding an audience, he rolled up the plans and gave his permission for that gentleman to be ushered into the royal presence.

Lord Alistair had managed to remain a friend of the touchy, sensitive prince by always being amiable, and always available to play cards, run races, gamble, or talk lighthearted nonsense.

He was always cautious to be as formal as possible. Other men, regarded as friends of the prince, had over-stepped the mark in the past by being too familiar and had fallen from royal favour.

'We heard you were in Brighton,' said the prince. 'What news?'

He waved a plump beringed hand to indicate that Lord Alistair had his permission to sit down. Lord Alistair was not feeling so easy in his mind as he had led Hannah to believe. The prince, with luck, would be amused. On the other hand, he might be furious.

'I have some gossip that concerns yourself, sire.'

'Indeed!' The royal face crumpled in displeasure.

'I trust it will amuse you.' Instead of telling the prince simply about Hannah's predicament in Brighton, Lord Alistair began at the beginning, describing the adventures of Miss Pym on the Exeter road, the Bath road, and the Portsmouth road, and the prince listened with delight. Even when he got to the real point of the story, Lord Alistair thought it politic to twist it slightly. He said the gossips had it that Miss Pym was not only a member of some foreign royal family, but besotted with the Prince of Wales.

The prince thought this was a famous joke. Lord Alistair had shrewdly guessed the touchy prince might not have found it so amusing if he had known that it was he who was said to be enamoured of Miss Pym.

'So now,' went on Lord Alistair, 'our poor Miss Pym cannot even leave her dwelling because of the vulgar crowd at her gate. I shall put the truth about.'

'Quite a character, this Miss Pym,' remarked the prince, in high good humour. 'Shall we see her?'

'I am escorting her to Lord Southern's ball. If it pleases Your Highness, I will point her out to you.'

'By all means.'

They talked of other things and then Lord Alistair took his leave. He had been just in time. The gossip about Miss Pym was being poured into the royal ears by all his cronies that evening, who were startled when the prince laughed and said he knew all about Miss Pym and was looking forward to meeting her at Lord Southern's ball.

The gossip about Hannah's true identity reached Monsieur Blanc the next morning, and shortly after that, Benjamin arrived, bearing the gown.

'I'm surprised you got the cheek to show your bleeding face in 'ere,' said the dressmaker.

'And I'm surprised you've got the cheek to look me in the eye,' said Benjamin, unruffled. 'You opened that trap o' yourn arter you swore not to. Did I mention you was nothing more but a common Englishman, wiff the emphasis on common? Nah. But I will now. So take this poxy dress and stuff–'

''Ere now!' cried Monsieur Blanc, alarmed. 'No need to be 'asty.'

Benjamin put the dress box down on a chair and made for the door.

'Did I say I wanted it back?' pleaded Monsieur Blanc. 'Did I now?'

Benjamin turned round, one eyebrow raised.

'Look, don't go around saying as how I'm plain Mr White or you'll ruin my trade. You can keep that there dress for the ball and bring it back next day. 'Ave we got a deal?'

Benjamin grinned. 'It's a deal.'

Mrs Cambridge's friends clustered around her, all mock sympathy. 'Poor Letitia. To be so misled by that charlatan. For Lord Alistair Munro knows the creature. He is even taking her to Lord Southern's ball! She is Miss Pym of nowhere in particular, or so I believe.'

Mrs Cambridge forced a light laugh. 'I knew she was common the minute I set eyes on her. But, my dears, you must forgive me. I could not help having a little fun at your expense. Of course, the silly creature is getting quite above herself with all the attention. I shall take pleasure in cutting her at the ball.' The friends, disappointed that they had not managed to tease her as they had hoped, vowed that they, too, would cut the dreadful Miss Pym, forgetting in their toadying to their social leader, Mrs Cambridge, that it is very hard to cut someone who does not know you from Adam.

4

When a woman isn't beautiful, people always say, 'You have lovely eyes, you have lovely hair.'

Anton Chekhov

Hannah found the very next day that the front of the house was free of sightseers. She went out for a walk, enjoying exploring the little dint-cobbled town with Benjamin behind her. They went for a long stroll along the chain pier, Hannah staring fascinated at the waves surging below. The sun was shining and brown-sailed boats were scudding before a brisk breeze.

'Do you think, Benjamin,' she called over her shoulder, 'that I should try sea bathing?'

'No, modom,' said Benjamin. 'I wouldn't go in that nasty stuff, not if you paid me.'

'But many ladies go sea bathing. And there is always an attendant. I should be in no danger of drowning.'

'You wouldn't get me in there,' said Benjamin with a shudder. 'Not ever.'

They had reached the end of the pier when Hannah saw Lady Beatrice approaching with her maid.

'I called at your home,' cried Lady Beatrice as she came up to her, 'and saw that the crowd had gone. Lord Alistair appears to have been successful.'

'Good for me,' said Hannah, 'but not for you. Has Sir Geoffrey found out yet that I am of no importance whatsoever?'

'Not yet. He will no doubt call on me as soon as he does.'

'When is this wedding to be, my lady?'

'In a month's time.'

'So soon?' Hannah was appalled.

'I am afraid so.'

They walked together along the pier. Behind Hannah came the sound of Benjamin's voice. He was obviously doing his best to impress Lady Beatrice's lady's maid. She hoped he was not regaling her with horrendous lies.

Lady Beatrice restrained an odd impulse to take Hannah's arm. She wondered why she felt so safe, so at ease with this Miss Pym.

Hannah was reflecting that masters and mistresses would be amazed if they knew how very alike in character they could be to their servants.

There was the care of Fanny, Mrs Clarence's lady's

maid. Hannah vividly remembered her. She had been a haughty, elegant creature, often mistaken for her mistress when she went out shopping. She was generally disliked by the other servants. There was an air of coldness about her which repelled all overtures of friendship. So she was damned as 'too hoity-toity' and suffered the consequent punishment handed out to hoity-toity servants. The footmen put spiders in her bed and the chambermaids put dye in her washing-up water.

And then Mrs Clarence had run away and Fanny's services were no longer required. Hannah had come across Fanny slowly packing her clothes, and had noticed that the lady's maid's fingers were trembling. Something had prompted Hannah to put a comforting arm about those rigid shoulders, and say, 'Whatever ails you can be helped, if only you will ask for help.' And Fanny had turned her face into Hannah's flat bosom and wept bitterly. It had come out that she would need to return home until she found another post. Her father was a drunken, violent brute and her mother little better, and Fanny was terrified. Hannah had immediately remembered a Mrs Jessingham, a friend of the absent Mrs Clarence, who had been complaining that she could not find a suitable lady's maid. So Hannah had taken Fanny to Mrs Jessingham and Mrs Jessingham had hired Fanny on the spot. Hannah had caught a glimpse of Fanny one day on one of her rare visits to London. Fanny looked grander and haughtier than ever. But then, Hannah thought, with a little sideways darting glance at Lady

Beatrice, perhaps, because of her parents, Fanny had built a brick wall around her to keep humanity at bay, and perhaps Lady Beatrice had done the same.

'I have no plans for the day,' said Lady Beatrice. 'I have been ordered to cultivate your society. Would it bore you too much to endure my company?'

'I would consider myself honoured,' said Hannah. 'But will it all not rebound on you when Sir Geoffrey finds out that I am Miss Pym of Nowhere?'

'I shall say I did not know,' said Lady Beatrice. 'In this life, it is very important to live in the minute, do you not think? Would you like my maid to bring you one of my ball gowns so that it may be altered?'

Hannah told her that Monsieur Blanc had been unexpectedly generous and had said she might have the gown for the night of the ball. 'I do not know how Benjamin managed it,' said Hannah uneasily. 'But he assured me he had told only the truth.'

'He is an unusual fellow,' commented Lady Beatrice. 'How warm it is today. We must make the most of it, for the English weather is so fickle, it could be snowing tomorrow.'

'I would like to go into the water.' Hannah stopped short and looked down at the surging sea.

Lady Beatrice laughed. 'Then why not?'

'The usual problem. I have nothing to wear.'

'Easily remedied. Marianne!' Lady Beatrice called over her shoulder. 'Run home and bring two flannel gowns and two caps and a quantity of towels and meet us by the bathing machines. I am sure Miss Pym will allow Benjamin to accompany you.'

Hannah was already rehearsing in her mind what she would say to Sir George Clarence when next they met. 'I went sea bathing in Brighton with Lady Beatrice Marsham.'

'I do not suppose Princess Caroline will be at the ball,' Hannah realized Lady Beatrice was saying. 'In Brighton, Mrs Fitzherbert is the wife, and you would think, to hear the gossips talk, that our prince had never even married Caroline of Brunswick.' She gave a bitter little laugh. 'At least I have something in common with Prinny; he loathes his wife and I loathed my husband and am well on my way to loathing another. The common people do not have to endure such miseries.'

'Oh, yes, they do,' said Hannah tartly. 'The baker's son may fall in love with a farm labourer's daughter, but he is not allowed to marry her, for she is far beneath him and he will be expected to marry a girl with a good-enough dowry so that his parents may expand their bakery, and so it goes on. It is money that makes the world go round. Romance is a rare luxury.' And having said that, Hannah thought of Sir George Clarence, so far above *her*, and felt quite dismal. Even if he were ruined and lost all his money and friends and ended up living in a hovel, there was the tremendous barrier of birth. 'But Mrs Fitzherbert is still the favourite,' she said, wrenching her thoughts back to the present. 'And surely that is love, for he did marry her, although the marriage is not recognized.'

'He has been philandering with Lady Jersey for some time,' said Lady Beatrice. 'When Princess

Caroline arrived on these shores for her wedding, the prince even sent Lady Jersey to meet her. But he keeps the connection with Mrs Fitzherbert.'

Hannah felt uncomfortable. She revered the prince and thought Lady Beatrice's conversation bordered on sedition.

To change the subject, she asked, 'Were you so very unhappy with your first husband?'

'To begin with.' Lady Beatrice gazed out to sea. 'You see, I was so young and so innocent and I found myself married to a drunk, a libertine, and a gamester. He tried his best to degrade me and nigh succeeded. Let us talk of something else.' Her face was cold and hard again.

'We are nearly at the bathing machines,' said Hannah nervously. 'Will the water be very cold, do you think?'

'Yes, very.'

'Then perhaps . . .'

'Courage, Miss Pym. It is a fine day and you must at least try. Here comes Marianne and your Benjamin.'

Soon Hannah found herself in a dark bathing machine with sand and seaweed on the floor. She undressed and put on the flannel gown and oilskin cap Lady Beatrice had lent her and then rapped on the door as a signal that she was ready. Then she sat down gingerly on the hard little bench at the back of the box as it began to roll forward, pulled by a strong farm horse.

When it stopped, Hannah stayed where she was,

cowering at the back of the box. The door of the bathing machine opened.

'Come along, madame,' said the bathing attendant, a large, burly woman. Hannah walked out on to the small platform at the front of the box. The horse stood patiently, little waves lapping against its legs. The bathing attendant took Hannah under the arms. 'Down you go,' she ordered. 'Nothing to fear. I'll have you safe.'

Hannah cast a wild look around. Lady Beatrice was already in the sea. She waved to Hannah. 'You will not drown,' she shouted. 'You can stand on the bottom. It is not deep here.'

Hannah allowed the attendant to lower her into the water. She gasped with shock as the icy sea flowed around her body. Then she felt ground under her feet. 'Are you all right?' asked the attendant.

'Yes,' said Hannah faintly. 'You may release me.'

The attendant removed her arms and Hannah stood still for a moment with her arms spread out to balance herself. Lady Beatrice moved towards her. 'Give me your hands,' she ordered. 'And then jump up and down. You will feel yourself floating.'

Hannah obediently did as ordered, feeling exhilarated as a large wave swept her to one side. She experienced a tremendous sense of freedom. Hannah had never followed the extremes of fashion that meant going around without stays. Now that she was used to the chill of the water, all she could feel was a marvellous sense of liberation. She began to laugh and jump up and down and splash the water with her hands. Lady Beatrice began to laugh as well and splashed water into Hannah's face. Hannah splashed water back until they were frolicking and yelling and shouting like schoolchildren.

'My lady is in trouble!' cried Marianne from the stony beach.

'She's laughing, that's all,' said Benjamin, sitting on a rock and smoking a cheroot.

'But my lady *never* laughs.' The little maid ran up and down on the shore like a worried terrier.

'Miss Pym makes life better for everyone,' said Benjamin. 'Look! They're both going in. I told you they was all right.'

The little maid came back to join him, smoothing down her dress and assuming the air of hauteur she had copied from her mistress. 'I must speak to my lady about her behaviour,' said Marianne, maintaining that fiction beloved of lady's maids the world over that they were able to remonstrate with their mistresses. 'An excess of emotion is vulgar.'

'That statue you works for,' said Benjamin laconically, 'could do with a bit of life.'

'I do not understand her behaviour,' mourned Marianne. 'She would not even let me assist her to undress.'

Hannah and Lady Beatrice at last joined them. Hannah's face was glowing. Her clothes were sticking to her salty body, and some sand had worked its way into one of her stockings, but she felt like Sir Francis Drake and every bit as bold.

'We had best return to our lodgings,' said Lady

Beatrice, 'and have warm baths. Salt water is so sticky.'

'I shall go tomorrow and tomorrow and tomorrow,' said Hannah dreamily, 'until I am able to swim like a fish.'

'Is that not your friend Lord Alistair?' asked Lady Beatrice. They had reached the promenade. Lady Beatrice pointed with her walking-cane.

Hannah looked and then stared. Lord Alistair Munro, as naked as the day he was born, was strolling nonchalantly towards the sea with a party of friends, all equally naked. He had a beautiful figure, tall and strong and athletic with broad shoulders, slim hips, and a trim waist.

'Come along, Miss Pym,' murmured Lady Beatrice, amused. 'We are not supposed to stand and stare, you know. When the gentlemen are in their buffs, we are not meant to know they even exist.'

'He is a very fine gentleman, a very *kind* gentleman,' said Hannah, averting her eyes and walking along beside Lady Beatrice.

Lady Beatrice did not reply. 'I mean,' pursued Hannah, 'it is very reassuring to know that there are kind and noble men in the world.'

'I do not believe in the existence of kind and noble men,' said Lady Beatrice, suddenly and savagely. 'They affect to be in love, but all have gross appetites. I am convinced that when Lord Alistair is not being charming to you, Miss Pym, he is off over the countryside, roistering with his friends, and seducing innocent girls.'

'You make all men in general and Lord Alistair in particular sound like villains in Haymarket plays,' commented Hannah.

'And fiction is based on fact.'

'Indeed! What then of the noble heroes?'

'Miss Pym, let us talk of something else or I shall become cross with you. Ah, here we are at your residence. May I call on you in, say, about an hour's time?'

'Gladly,' replied Hannah, suddenly wishing that Lord Alistair could see Lady Beatrice in that moment, as she stood at the gate, the stiff breeze tugging at her muslin skirts, one hand holding her bonnet, her cheeks pink and her large eyes sparkling.

Hannah went indoors to instruct Benjamin on his duties, the first of which was filling a bath. And Hannah took her first bath naked. Like most ladies, she usually wore a shift so that the sight of her own body should not bring a blush to her cheeks. But now it seemed perfectly natural to lie in the water stark naked and not feel ashamed. Sea bathing, mused Hannah dreamily, was almost *pagan*. It changed one's mind about all sorts of things. She wondered if she could find the courage to go about without stays.

She had no sooner dressed again than Lord Alistair Munro called to tell her of his success with the Prince of Wales. He was on the point of telling Hannah also that it might not be a good idea for her to appear at the ball. Brighton society blamed her for tricking it and he knew several ladies who would go out of their way to be nasty to her, but Hannah looked so elated, so happy at the idea of going that he did not have the heart to dim her pleasure.

'Lady Beatrice Marsham,' announced Benjamin in the strangulated and refined tones he used for polite company.

Lady Beatrice sailed in. She was wearing a modish bonnet with a high crown and a striped silk gown which flattered her excellent figure. She looked slightly taken aback to see Lord Alistair and Hannah noticed the shutter coming down over her eyes.

'Lord Alistair has been to see the prince,' cried Hannah, 'and all is well. His Highness was vastly amused and not cross at all!'

'Then you must have charmed him,' said Lady Beatrice to Lord Alistair.

He laughed. 'I was diplomacy at its best, I assure you,' he said.

'I had my first dip in the sea, my lord,' said Hannah proudly, 'and would not have dared had not Lady Beatrice elected to join me. It was the most liberating experience. I felt quite *wanton*!'

Lady Beatrice looked at Hannah with affection and Lord Alistair studied her curiously. Why had the haughty Lady Beatrice stooped to be kind to the undistinguished Miss Pym?

Hannah rang the bell and ordered Benjamin to bring in tea and cakes.

'But we haven't got no cakes, modom,' said Benjamin in injured tones.

'Then run and get them,' snapped Hannah, thinking, not for the first time, that Benjamin had a lot to learn.

'Stay!' said Lord Alistair, holding up his hand. 'Allow me to entertain you ladies at a pastry cook's. There is a very good one near the pier, where we may sit and look out of the window at the waves.'

Lady Beatrice opened her mouth to refuse. But her eyes fell on Hannah, who looked like a child at Christmas and the refusal died on her lips.

Soon they were seated at a small round table at the bay window of the pastry cook's. Hannah looked out at the fluttering muslins and fringed parasols of the ladies and the military strut of their gallants and beyond them to the magnificence of the restless sea. Her eyes glittered with tears and Lady Beatrice put out an impulsive hand. 'What ails you, Miss Pym?'

Hannah took out a small but serviceable handkerchief and dried her eyes. 'I was thinking of Sir George Clarence,' she said.

'Is he dead?' Lady Beatrice looked anxious.

'Oh, no.' Hannah shook her head. 'Sir George Clarence took me to tea at Gunter's in Berkeley Square. It was the most wonderful thing that had ever happened to me. I can still hear the chink of china and smell the confectionery . . .'

'Of course you can,' teased Lady Beatrice. 'Are you not in a pastry cook's?'

Hannah shook her head. 'I was thinking how much my life has changed since that very day. I was thinking how very happy I am and I was praying that both of you could be as happy.'

Lord Alistair looked surprised. 'You underrate the

charms of your company, Miss Pym. I am having a delightful time.'

A shadow fell across Lady Beatrice's face and she studied the table. For she was suddenly and sharply aware that she had been enjoying herself that very day as she had never enjoyed a day since her late husband had led her to the altar. To her horror, tears welled up in her own eyes, and she brushed them angrily away.

Lord Alistair looked at her curiously. He had already damned her as a hard, cold bitch, devoid of feeling. Now all he could see was a beautiful woman in distress. Something tugged at his heart, but his mind told him angrily that Lady Beatrice was an experienced flirt and probably a good actress.

'Getting like a wake,' said Benjamin. Hannah sharply reproved him for impertinence, but Lord Alistair laughed and said, 'That man of yours must have Scotch blood in him. No one can rival Scotch servants for speaking their minds.'

But Benjamin's remark had the effect of lightening the atmosphere. Lord Alistair told them a story of two friends of the prince's who had bet on a couple of geese to see which one would cross the road first. A certain Mr Rothmere won the bet and was so grateful to his winning bird that he adopted it and took it everywhere with him on a lead, just like a dog.

Lady Beatrice capped that by telling a story of her visit to a ladies' gambling club in London, and how the women turned their pelisses and spencers inside out before playing, imitating the men who wore their coats inside out for luck, and how all had played with the same intensity as their male counterparts, until a Lady James had won a great deal of money and one of her opponents accused her of cheating. Lady James had snatched off that opponent's cap and jumped on it, and so a regular battle had broken out, with women screaming and tearing each other's hair and gowns.

She had just finished her story when she glanced out of the window and saw Sir Geoffrey and his mother walking past. She shrank back in her seat. Lord Alistair twisted his head and looked to see what had frightened her. He recognized Sir Geoffrey.

'That was your fiancé, I think,' he said to Lady Beatrice. 'Would you like me to call him?'

'No, that is not necessary,' said Lady Beatrice. 'I shall no doubt see him this evening. I must go. No, do not rise, Miss Pym. You have not finished your tea.'

She hurried out, with her maid scurrying after her.

'Now, what was all that about?' Lord Alistair gave Hannah a quizzical look.

'Oh, my lord,' said Hannah earnestly, 'I am sore worried about dear Lady Beatrice. She is being constrained to marry a monster.'

'Impossible! She is a widow of independent means.'

Hannah shook her head. 'You see, Blackstone left her nothing but debts. Her parents paid them and settled a comfortable income on her, but she has had only a year to enjoy her freedom. If she does not marry Sir Geoffrey, then her parents say they will cut her off without a shilling.'

'How very Gothic,' he commented drily. 'Are you sure you are not being gulled?'

'No, my lord. I am a good judge of character. Servants must be good judges of character, you know, for they are always being subjected to the whims of their employer or his guests. I got to know which ladies to be wary of. Once one of Mrs Clarence's guests insisted on giving me two sovereigns. The following day she lost heavily at cards, and instead of just asking me for the money back, she told Mrs Clarence I had stolen money from her and demanded that my room be searched.'

'Which Mrs Clarence did?'

'Which Mrs Clarence did not. The guest was told to leave immediately.'

'I wish I had met this Mrs Clarence,' said Lord Alistair.

Hannah clasped her hands. 'You would have liked her above all things, my lord. So gay and pretty and happy.'

'And yet she ran off with a footman?'

'Well, you know, he was a very handsome footman and a happy fellow, not much in the common way of footmen any more than my Benjamin is. I mean he was not vain or lazy. I believe – I hope – he truly loved her. And, do you see, Mr Clarence was so morose and withdrawn and given to criticizing her constantly. Yes, she did a wicked thing, but I cannot find it in my heart to blame her for it.'

'Do you know where she is now?'

Hannah shook her head. 'I often hope when I am on my travels to meet her.'

'Would you recognize her? She may be vastly changed.'

Hannah looked stubborn. 'I would know her anywhere.'

'Your loyalty does you credit, as does your strange loyalty to Lady Beatrice.'

'I like her and I wish I could help her,' said Hannah. Her odd eyes flashed green as she studied Lord Alistair Munro from his guinea-gold curls to his embroidered waistcoat. 'But *you* could surely help her, my lord.'

'I? Fan me, ye winds! What on earth could *I* do?'

Hannah gripped the edge of the table and said in a measured voice, 'You could marry her yourself, my lord.'

His blue eyes were icy and his voice cold as he said, 'You forget yourself, Miss Pym. Pray talk of something else.'

Hannah blushed and looked so downcast that he felt as if he had just slapped a child. 'Forgive me for being so harsh,' he said gently, 'but your recent successes in matchmaking may have gone to your head. I am that rarest of creatures, a genuinely happy bachelor. Were I not, I would still not look with any affection on such as Lady Beatrice, a cruel and heartless flirt.'

Hannah began to talk of other things and was happy that by the time he had taken his leave of her, he appeared to have forgotten her unfortunate remark.

That evening, Sir Geoffrey strode up and down Lady Beatrice's drawing-room in a fury. 'And so I find this

Miss Pym is some undistinguished female with no connections whatsoever. You are not to see her again, d'ye hear?'

Lady Beatrice let the piece of embroidery she had been working on fall to her lap. 'You may constrain me to marry you, Sir Geoffrey, but I shall choose my own friends until we are married.'

'Your parents shall hear of this, madam. Ho, yes. They will hear you are lowering yourself to common company.'

Lady Beatrice picked up her embroidery again and set a careful stitch. 'I do not think Miss Pym at all common. She is full of surprises and has powerful friends. By all means tell my parents. I shall tell them in turn that you ordered me to befriend her with a view to getting a title. Now, my parents are after your money, as you very well know, but they are high sticklers, and although my ancestors got the title in the first place by ignoble means, they would not look kindly on your machinations.'

'They are so anxious to get their hands on my money, they would put up with anything,' said Sir Geoffrey brutally. 'You'd best pack your traps and come back to Mother's.'

'Oh, no.' Lady Beatrice looked at him coldly. 'You are among my servants now, Sir Geoffrey, and I have only to call for help if you hold a gun to my head. I was a fool to go with you before, for I realize now, I am of no interest to you dead.'

He grinned at her. 'You forget, sweeting, that if you do not do what I ask, I shall simply break off the engagement and your parents will cast you off just as if you had broken it.'

'I thought of that,' remarked Lady Beatrice evenly. She selected a thread of purple silk and held it against the cloth, her head a little on one side. 'My parents, as you so rightly point out, are anxious to get your money, and believe me, they are even more ruthless than you. Should you terminate this engagement, or try to, they would drag you through the courts. They would sue you for breach of promise. My parents love the courts. My father's lawyers spend most of their time there, suing people over boundaries and tenancies. They would make your life a misery.'

'They would not dare!'

'You *have* met my parents, have you not? Ah, that gives you pause. You know I have the right of it. I shall continue to see Miss Pym. She makes me laugh. Good night, Sir Geoffrey!'

Lord Alistair Munro came across a party of acquaintances on the front the following day. They had telescopes trained on the ladies' bathing machines.

Lord Alistair looked to see what the focus of their interest was. He had very good eyesight, and even without a telescope he recognized Lady Beatrice and Miss Pym in the water. They were splashing about like seals and their laughter faintly reached his ears. And then, as he watched, Lady Beatrice, with the help of the attendant, climbed out of the water up the short wooden ladder to the bathing machine. Her gown was moulded to her body. He felt a quickening of his senses, and suddenly impatient with himself, he turned abruptly and began to walk away.

Miss Hannah Pym, without stays, ventured to take a walk, with Benjamin behind her, later that day. Lady Beatrice had had a summons from her parents, who had arrived in Brighton.

The feel of her own unrestricted body seemed somehow sinful, and Hannah felt she had gone too far. In fact, her thin, flat-chested figure looked just the same as it did when held by a long corset, but Hannah, although wearing a smart blue wool gown under a pelisse, for the day had turned chilly, was sure everyone was staring at her and everyone knew she had thrown off her stays.

She chided herself and told herself not to be ridiculous, but she was uneasily aware of hard glances cast in her direction. It came as almost a relief to see Mrs Cambridge approaching her with a party of ladies. But the welcoming smile died on Hannah's lips as Mrs Cambridge came straight up to her and said haughtily, 'You are an impostor and a charlatan. Do not have the temerity to appear at Southern's ball or it will be the worse for you.'

Then she minced on, her friends casting many angry glances back at Hannah.

'Cats!' said Benjamin. But Hannah stood stock-still, a wave of misery flooding her. She had so wanted to go to that ball, but now she could not. The wind was rising and little grey clouds were scudding across the sun and the sea had a restless, angry look. At one corner of the street, a ballad-seller was singing 'Death and the Lady Margaret's Ghost', and at the other corner, another ballad-seller was competing by singing 'Chevy Chase'. Their voices rose and fell on the wind, sometimes a cacophony, sometimes in unexpected unison as they both hit the same note.

Hannah turned about and went slowly back to her lodgings. She left Benjamin to make tea and went to her bedchamber and put on her stays, feeling obscurely that God had sent Mrs Cambridge to punish the wanton.

Later, in the parlour, seated in front of a bright fire of sea coal, Hannah said dismally, 'You may as well take a letter to Sir Alistair and tell him I cannot go to that ball, Benjamin.'

'You got to go, modom,' said Benjamin. 'The prince will be there. Think o' that? Ain't that worth putting up wiff a few old cats, mouthing an' staring? Lady Beatrice'll be there and Lord Alistair is a friend o' the prince's, ain't he? Well!'

Hannah leaned her head on her hand and stared into the flames. Although not a very religious woman, she felt that she was flying in the face of Providence by moving out of her class. Once a servant, always a servant. One had to accept one's station in life, however low, for that was where the Good Lord had put one.

'If you don't go,' said Benjamin anxiously, 'then *I* can't go and I'll never get to see the prince, not ever!'

Hannah, lost in her own worried thoughts, did not hear him. Was she such a bad woman? Look at the matches she had made on her first three journeys. Had she not brought happiness to others? Was Mrs Cambridge such a saint, such a fine woman, that Hannah Pym should shrink before her snubs and be terrified at the thought of receiving more? Was she to sit here on the night of the ball, before this very fire, hearing the music in her head, seeing the prince only in her mind's eye? She straightened up. 'I shall go,' she said quietly.

'Knowed I could talk you out of the megrims,' said Benjamin, and went off to make more tea.

Lady Beatrice faced her parents. They were seated opposite her in her drawing-room, side by side on a backless sofa, ramrod-straight. Her father, the earl, was a tall man who still wore his hair powdered. He had pale, cold eyes, set rather close together, and a large hooked nose. His countess was small and plump with fine eyes in a crumpled, discontented face. They were listening intently to their daughter.

'So you see,' Lady Beatrice was saying, 'this son-in-law you have picked out held me up at gunpoint on the Brighton road and forced me into his carriage.'

The countess flicked open a small gold snuff-box and helped herself to a delicate pinch. 'Such passion,' she commented in a thin voice. 'Very headstrong man, but the strength of his feelings for you does him credit.'

'Fiddlesticks,' said Lady Beatrice. 'Are my feelings not to be taken into consideration? I despise and detest the man.'

'From my observation,' commented her father, 'I have noticed you despise and detest all men.'

'Perhaps my feelings for the opposite sex might have been warmer had you not seen fit to marry me off to a lecher and wastrel,' snapped Lady Beatrice.

'Oh, Blackstone?' The countess shrugged. 'An unfortunate rip. But he's dead now. No, no, do not plague us with more protestations. You are still of an age to breed and we need an heir. Sir Geoffrey will do very well.'

Lady Beatrice surveyed her parents, wondering if there was anything she could say that would move them, wondering if there had ever been anything she could have said to spark some parental feeling from them. But they had had little do with her from the day she was born. She had been turned over to a wet-nurse, then a nanny, then a governess, then sent to a seminary. She remembered returning from the seminary to find a houseful of guests and hearing her father ask a footman, 'Who is that very pretty young lady? One of our guests?' And the footman's reply, 'No, my lord, it is Lady Beatrice.'

That evening, for the first time, she had been asked to dine with her parents instead of taking her meal in the schoolroom. They had plied her with questions as to her talents – could she play the pianoforte, were her water-colours passable? – and, flushed and happy under all this sudden attention, Lady Beatrice had chattered away, elated to sense she had done something at last to bring herself to the attention of her parents. She was to learn all too soon that it was her looks that had caused this sudden interest – looks that could be traded profitably on the marriage market.

'So,' she said bleakly, 'you are still determined to turn me off should I not marry Sir Geoffrey?'

'Oh, yes,' said the countess, 'but you will not do anything silly. Do we not give you a generous allowance for your clothes and jewels? You are our child and will not do anything to turn yourself into a pauper.'

'I might put it to the test,' said Lady Beatrice slowly. 'Have you both thought of your reputations if I should end in the workhouse?'

'Yes,' said her father, 'and it is fortunate you have been so thoroughly nasty to so many. No one would care. In fact, society might take a malicious delight in the spectacle of the haughty Lady Beatrice being humbled.'

'Leave me,' said Lady Beatrice wearily.

Both rose. 'We shall go ahead with the arrangements for the wedding,' said the countess. 'A quiet affair, of course.'

When they had gone, Lady Beatrice sat feeling a lump rising in her throat. Her father had said, 'No one would care,' and that had hurt dreadfully, and then she thought of Hannah Pym. Miss Pym liked her, she was sure of that. Miss Pym would listen to her. Perhaps there was something Miss Pym could do.

She went alone to Hannah's, without her maid, feeling she could not trust her own servants to be loyal to her. If Marianne came with her, Marianne would hear the conversation and might report it to the other servants and one of those servants might report what she said to her parents.

Hannah was surprised but pleased to see Lady Beatrice and led her through to the parlour, where the fire still burned brightly.

'It is an odd time of night to be making a call,' said Lady Beatrice, handing her pelisse and walking-cane and gloves to Benjamin.

'You are always welcome,' said Hannah. 'Benjamin, you may have the evening off.'

Benjamin glanced at the clock. Ten in the evening. 'No, thank you, modom,' he said.

'I am asking you to take yourself off,' said Hannah crossly. 'If you do not wish to go out, then go to your room.'

Hannah wanted rid of Benjamin. She noticed the strain in Lady Beatrice's face and knew she must want to talk privately.

Benjamin decided to go out. His fingers closed over the dice he kept in his pocket. He knew Hannah disapproved of his gambling, but he was determined his mistress should cut a dash in Brighton society and he knew she would need money to do that. He would not gamble much. Just get enough to hire a carriage and pair. Benjamin's eyes gleamed. He felt his mistress should not be seen walking everywhere in Brighton.

Hannah offered Lady Beatrice tea, which she refused, and then asked her gently if there was anything troubling her.

Lady Beatrice, wondering why she had called,

feeling no one could help her now, said she merely had come on an impulse and had not realized the hour was so late. She rose to go.

'No, I pray you,' said Hannah, 'do not leave. I am used to late hours. I am an odd companion for you, am I not? I have an undistinguished background and an undistinguished appearance. I wish my nose were straight and my vowels flawless.'

Lady Beatrice surveyed her. 'You have very fine eyes, Miss Pym, a wealth of kindness, and a distinguished soul.'

'You are kind. Most ladies of your caste would immediately shun me.'

Lady Beatrice sat down again and slowly removed her bonnet. 'What were your parents like, Miss Pym?'

'Perpetually worried, old before their time,' said Hannah ruefully. 'I left home very young and saw little of them after that. They died in a smallpox epidemic, as did my brothers and sisters. Mrs Clarence, my late employer's wife, paid for their funerals.'

'Did they give you affection?'

Hannah thought sadly of the damp basement in which she had been brought up. 'They did not have much time for affection,' she said. 'They were very poor, and poverty does not allow much leisure for finer feelings. I gather, somehow, that you have just seen your parents.'

'Yes, this very evening.'

'And do they show any signs of relenting?'

'No, not a whit.'

'Have they considered that, should you not go ahead with this marriage and they carry out their threat, society will consider them monsters?'

Lady Beatrice gave a thin smile. 'They pointed out, quite rightly, that I have alienated the affections of all. They have the right of it. I have hit out left and right because of my own misery and now must pay the price of being friendless.'

'Except for me,' said Hannah quietly. 'Except for me.'

'Miss Pym, I am deeply indebted to you. There! I declare you have made me cry.'

Tears rolled down Lady Beatrice's cheeks and she fumbled in her sleeve for a handkerchief.

Hannah leaned forward and patted her hand. 'It will do you good to cry,' she said.

'I – I f-feel so weak,' sobbed Lady Beatrice. She dried her eyes and blew her nose. 'I should be stronger. Surely I could earn some money, find a post as a governess.'

'I think the life of a scullery maid is better than that of a governess,' said Hannah. 'Poor creatures. They are neither fish nor fowl. They are despised by master and servants alike. I have it! You can live with me!'

Lady Beatrice stared at her.

'Why not?' Hannah's eyes were golden. 'We should have to live very simply, you know. I plan to retire to some little cottage in the country. I meant to make a few more stage-coach journeys, but there is more to life than travelling. Just think, Lady Beatrice! You would perhaps find it tedious, but you would be free.'

'Free,' echoed Lady Beatrice, looking at Hannah almost shyly. 'Why should you do this for me?'

'Because we are friends, are we not?'

'I could, you know,' said Lady Beatrice, her large eyes beginning to sparkle. 'How long have you rented this place for?'

'Only three weeks.'

'Splendid. You can move in with me, and . . . oh, let me see . . . I will need to give my servants notice . . . and . . . and I have a great quantity of jewels. We could sell those and have enough to keep us comfortably. Why did I never think of that? Oh, Miss Pym. The prison gates are opening at last. And I always thought I was a strong person. I could have done this before, or as soon as I heard about the planned wedding to Sir Geoffrey. It is all so simple. I do not need a carriage or jewels. Yes, I have a carriage of my own in London, although my parents hold the title deeds of my house there. I can sell both carriage and horses. What a vast amount of money we society people do spend. If I do not need to keep up appearances I can be quite comfortable. I do not even need to go to the Southerns' ball.'

A shadow crossed Hannah's face. 'Oh, do go to this one ball, Lady Beatrice . . . for me. For Mrs Cambridge met me this day and told me not to go or it would be the worse for me, but I do want to see the prince.'

'Then I shall go with you, and in my company, the Mrs Cambridges of Brighton will steer clear. When can you move in with me?'

'Tomorrow,' said Hannah. 'But I must get Benjamin to take a letter to Lord Alistair telling him of my new address or he will not know where to fetch me for the ball.'

'Ah, Lord Alistair,' said Lady Beatrice thoughtfully. 'I feel that one does not approve of me.'

'I am sure you are mistaken,' said Hannah firmly. She looked at the now flushed and radiant Lady Beatrice. Lord Alistair, thought Hannah, disapproved of the old Lady Beatrice. But perhaps, just perhaps, he could be encouraged to fall in love with the new model . . .

5

I prithee send me back my heart,
Since I cannot have thine:
For if from yours you will not part,
Why then shouldst thou have mine?

Sir John Suckling

Benjamin, to Hannah's surprise, was not pleased that they were to move into Lady Beatrice's household. She thought he would have been delighted to be part of an aristocrat's staff. But Benjamin said he was her footman and her footman alone and he would not take part in any other work in Lady Beatrice's establishment.

'You are too nice,' said Hannah crossly. 'Lady Beatrice is giving all her staff their marching orders and so you will soon be the sole servant again. Now as to the matter of the rent. Where is this Mr Barnstable? He surely wants to be paid something.'

'Not he,' said Benjamin. 'Just you pack your things, modom, and leave Mr Barnstable to me.'

Benjamin went out in search of Mr Barnstable or Captain Barnstable or Colonel Barnstable, for he was sure he was a military man.

The rank turned out to be that of captain, as Benjamin soon discovered when he finally ran that gentleman to earth in the Ship Tavern. 'I'd better count the silver,' said the captain, getting to his feet.

'Don't you dare!' said Benjamin shrilly. 'If you got any complaints, you will find my lady resident with Lady Beatrice Marsham, and you'll find that hutch of yourn a damned sight cleaner than it was when we moved in.'

'You're a mountebank,' sneered the captain, 'and that mistress of yours is no better. Foreign royalty indeed. I heard all about that trick.'

Benjamin removed his white gloves and struck the captain across the cheek with them.

The captain reeled back, horrified. His friends stared at Benjamin, outraged. 'Have you run mad?' gasped the captain. 'I don't duel with *servants*.' He turned to his friends. 'Here, help me drop this hothead off the end of the pier.'

Rough hands seized Benjamin and carried him out. He fought and struggled as he was borne remorselessly towards the pier.

Benjamin finally ceased to struggle and lay inert in their hands, but his brain was working furiously. 'Hey!' he cried out suddenly. 'Ain't that disgraceful? Imagine a lady going into the water without a stitch on.'

He was dropped unceremoniously on to the pier while his captors rushed to the edge and stared wildly in the direction of the bathing machines, crying, 'Where? Where?'

But the day was cold and there was nothing to be seen and when they turned back the nimble figure of the footman was running hell for leather off the pier.

Lord Alistair Munro was surprised to receive a letter from Miss Pym in which she said she had moved in with Lady Beatrice. He felt Miss Pym was being duped in some way. He was sure Lady Beatrice had some ulterior motive and refused to believe she was being forced into marriage. But there was another surprise in store for him. On the day of the ball, an announcement appeared in the local paper to the effect that the engagement between Lady Beatrice Marsham and Sir Geoffrey Handford was at an end. He studied it for some time and then came to the conclusion that it was merely Lady Beatrice playing her old game but worse than before. She had rejected Sir Geoffrey in a public and humiliating way.

Lady Beatrice's enraged parents called to find she was out walking with Miss Pym. Sir Geoffrey and his mother called, to be told she was 'not at home'.

By evening, both Hannah and Lady Beatrice were secretly wishing they did not have to go to the ball. Hannah was sure she would be dreadfully insulted by one and all, and Lady Beatrice was sure Sir Geoffrey would make a public scene.

But she was deeply indebted to Hannah Pym and

could not bring herself to let that lady go on her own. Admittedly Hannah was being escorted by Lord Alistair, but Lady Beatrice knew Hannah needed the support of another woman. Lord Alistair could dance with Hannah only twice and that left acres of evening in which she could be attacked.

After her maid had dressed her, Lady Beatrice went to Hannah's room and found to her amusement that Benjamin was trying to persuade his mistress to wear pink feathers in her hair. How he had come by the feathers, Hannah did not know, but she could not get him to listen when she protested that pink feathers would look ridiculous with a gold silk gown.

'You must wear jewels, Miss Pym,' said Lady Beatrice. 'We shall both go armoured in my best jewellery.' She herself was wearing a blue silk gown with a fairy-tale tiara of sapphires and diamonds on her black hair. She sent Marianne to fetch a diamond tiara and diamond necklace and then stood back to survey the effect as the necklace was placed around Hannah's neck and the tiara on her sandy hair.

'Very grand,' she said at last. 'You'll do. Just look at all the jewels I have, Miss Pym. We will be able to live in great comfort. There are some pieces which belong to the Debrens and which must go back to my parents, but the rest are very fine and should fetch a good sum.'

Hannah was dazzled as she looked at her own reflection in the mirror. Who could snub a lady dressed in such magnificence? If only Sir George Clarence could see her now!

Then a shadow crossed her face. Lady Beatrice was now to be her friend and companion, the beautiful, the magnetic Lady Beatrice. Would Sir George be able to look on such a lady and keep heart-whole? A stab of jealousy hit Hannah and in that moment she thought of Lord Alistair Munro, so carefree, so single, so marriageable. Were he to fall in love with Lady Beatrice, all her troubles would be over, and Hannah would be free to see Sir George again without this dangerous beauty in tow.

Lord Alistair arrived promptly at eight o'clock and seemed to take it in good part that he was expected to escort Lady Beatrice as well.

'I saw the announcement of the end of your engagement in the newspaper,' he said, 'so I assume your parents are reconciled to your single state. Miss Pym told me some Gothic tale that they would cut you off without a penny.'

Lady Beatrice went over to an escritoire in the corner of the drawing-room, took out a letter and handed it to him, saying, 'This has just arrived.'

He raised his quizzing-glass and studied it, his thin eyebrows rising in surprise. It was from her father, the earl.

Dear Beatrice *[read Lord Alistair]*, I do not call you daughter, for you are no longer a daughter of mine. Your disobedience and folly are beyond words. Perhaps you think I will not carry out my threat? Then I take leave to tell you I have written to my bankers to cancel your allowance and given instructions to my agents to put your London house on the market. If you do not come to your senses, then you will end up on the streets, and may the Lord have mercy on your wicked soul.

Yrs, Debren.

'And how will you manage?' he asked, putting the letter down.

'I am to be Miss Pym's companion,' said Lady Beatrice gaily. 'We are to reside in a cottage in the country and be very rustic. Oh, I wish I had thought of this before.'

'Life in a cottage for such as you can be a dismal affair.' Lord Alistair looked at her cynically. 'No more parties or balls or hearts to break.'

Lady Beatrice gave a brittle laugh. 'I know you have a low opinion of me, my lord, but pray forget it for this one evening – Miss Pym's evening.'

Hannah felt very elated as she was helped into Lord Alistair's open carriage, very conscious of the glitter of diamonds at her neck and on her head. The day had been dark and dismal, but now a low sun was sinking into the sea, the air was still and balmy, and the restless sea-gulls of Brighton screamed overhead.

The journey to Lord Southern's house was only a few yards, in fact; they queued from Lady Beatrice's house to the entrance of Lord Southern's mansion rather than drove, but then, one must never arrive on foot.

All Hannah's elation suddenly crumbled. For as they descended from the carriage, helped down by

Benjamin, resplendent in gold-and-black livery – where did he get it? wondered Hannah – here was Mrs Cambridge, and beside her, her friends, just arriving.

They stood and stared at Hannah and then began to titter and giggle maliciously. 'Pay them no heed,' urged Lady Beatrice. But Benjamin was suddenly in front of Mrs Cambridge and her group, a Benjamin white-faced, eyes aglitter, hands clenched. 'Wot you staring at, you bleedin' harpies, you rotten scum o' the kennel, you daughters o' whores!'

'BENJAMIN!' shrieked Hannah.

But his outburst had the desired effect. Clucking like a party of outraged hens, Mrs Cambridge and her friends scuttled quickly into the mansion.

'That footman is disgraceful,' said Lady Beatrice to Lord Alistair. 'You should be taking him to task, not standing there giggling.'

'True,' he said with a grin. 'How very true. But how refreshing to hear someone say what one would not dare say oneself.'

'I shall speak to you later, Benjamin,' said Hannah. 'I have a good mind to send you away.'

Benjamin looked unrepentant as he doggedly followed them up the carpeted stairs. He was determined to wait in the hall with the other footmen so that he might have a good view of the Prince of Wales when he arrived.

Lady Beatrice and Hannah left their shawls in an ante-room, as if oblivious of the frosty stares from all the ladies present. But as they walked up the stairs,

Lady Beatrice said ruefully, 'We must be prepared to take the wall this evening, for none will dare dance with us.'

But there were young gentlemen there who had never heard of Lady Beatrice's hard-hearted reputation, and soon she was being solicited to dance.

Lord Alistair stood up with Hannah for the first country dance, but was curiously aware of every step that Lady Beatrice took. She looked younger, he thought. Perhaps with parents such as she possessed, there was much to be said in her defence. Mindful of his duties to his partner, he made sure he engaged Hannah for supper, and then, when the dance was over, led her to one of the gilt seats around the ballroom before going off to talk to his friends.

'Of course, it is not Almack's,' said a dowager loudly beside Hannah, 'so I suppose one must expect to have to rub shoulders with all sorts of peculiar people.' Hannah knew this remark was intended for her own ears and was sorry that the reprehensible Benjamin was far away in the hall.

And then, as the cotillion which was being performed finally finished, a rustling and murmuring started up in the room. The Prince of Wales had arrived.

Lord Alistair came up to Hannah and held out his hand and then led her into the line that was being formed to greet the prince. Hannah steeled herself to forget the nastiness of her tormentors. This was a moment to treasure.

The Prince of Wales entered. He was fat and florid, his hair teased and curled all over his head, and his watery blue eyes looking haughtily about. Lord Alistair realized that the prince was in a bad humour and wished suddenly he had not brought Hannah. Although the prince had been amused by Lord Alistair's account of events, he had the fault of believing only the last person who spoke to him. Lord Alistair had a sinking feeling that some malicious gossip had given the prince an unflattering picture of this Miss Pym.

The prince came down the line, stopping here and there to exchange a few words, followed by Lord Southern. He came to a halt in front of Lord Alistair, looked at Hannah and at the sparkle of her diamonds, and said, 'That female ain't here, is she?'

In a colourless voice, Lord Alistair said, 'May I present Miss Hannah Pym, Your Highness.'

Hannah sank into a court curtsy. The prince scowled down at her. Hannah raised her eyes to his. The prince saw they were full of tears. 'Why do you cry, hey?' he snapped.

'Oh, sire,' said Hannah Pym. 'I am overcome with emotion. This night I have met England.'

The scowl left the prince's face, for in Hannah's eyes was simple adoration and that was something the touchy, oversensitive prince was not used to seeing in the eyes of his subjects. He forgot that he had recently heard that this Miss Pym was as common as the barber's chair and had been putting about that he was in love with her. His fat cheeks creased in a flattered smile and he slowly held out his arm.

There was a little gasp, someone let out a slow hiss

of surprise, and the dazed Hannah took the royal arm and was led forward. At the head of the line, the prince turned and faced Hannah. 'Now you can tell everyone you walked with royalty,' he said indulgently.

'If I could die now,' said Hannah fervently, 'I would die happy. I have long worshipped you from afar, sire.'

'Tol-rol!' said the prince dismissively, but highly delighted. 'We are pleased to meet a lady of such character and breeding.' He signalled to his friends and courtiers, who clustered around him as he was led away. Lady Jenks, a friend of Mrs Cambridge, whispered in her ear, 'Did you hear *that*? Do you not think now the original rumour was true? He called her a lady of character and breeding. And look at the way her footman dared to abuse us!'

Hannah sat down again by the edge of the ballroom in a happy daze. The dowager beside her smiled and said, 'I have not had the pleasure of your acquaintance. Miss Pym, is it not?'

But before Hannah could reply, she found she was being asked to dance by Lord Southern himself, Lord Southern who had only given her two fingers to shake on her arrival, and yet who now seemed to wish to mark her out for special attention.

Hannah was still wrapped in rosy clouds of glory. The only thing that marred her pleasure was that she was a childless spinster. What a tale to tell grandchildren before a winter's fire! She did not even notice that Lord Alistair had taken Lady Beatrice on to the floor.

Lord Alistair had noticed that Sir Geoffrey Hand-ford, who had arrived late, was approaching Lady Beatrice in a threatening way, and something had moved him to prevent her from being faced with a nasty scene. The dance was another country one and took quite half an hour to perform, and Lord Alistair had the satisfaction of seeing Sir Geoffrey stride off to the card-room.

There was not much opportunity for conversation during the figures of the dance, but afterwards, as was the custom, Lord Alistair promenaded with Lady Beatrice round the floor.

'Our Miss Pym is in high alt,' said Lady Beatrice. 'What did she say to make our sulky Prinny take such a liking to her?'

'She treated him with all the reverence normally accorded to a saint and he reacted favourably. It is now being said that Miss Pym *must* be foreign royalty. That lady attracts adventures, so beware.'

'If by adventures you mean distress and danger, I hope her days of adventuring are over. Goodness, this ballroom is hot. They have enough candles to light the Vatican.'

'There is a balcony at the end which overlooks the sea, if you would care for a breath of air.'

'Gladly.'

They walked together to the end of the room and found themselves on a small balcony facing the sea. A small moon was shining on the sea and the susurration of the waves rising and falling on the beach reached their ears.

Lady Beatrice put her hands on the railing of the balcony and looked out. 'How very peaceful it is,' she said, half to herself. 'If only I could leave now. Sir Geoffrey, I feel, is determined to seek me out and make a scene.'

'I do not think he can do that with the prince present. It is well known he craves a title higher than that of knight and will do nothing to bring the royal wrath down on his head. How did he come by his knighthood? Stealing money from Indian potentates hardly counts as gallantry.'

'I assume he came by it as most men do in these venal days,' said Lady Beatrice. 'He probably paid vast sums of money to people in the right quarters.' She turned and glanced back into the ballroom. 'I wonder if I shall miss all this,' she said. 'Just at this moment, freedom is so sweet that I doubt it.'

'And Miss Pym will be company enough?'

'I am sure of it.'

'And will you then cease to flirt? Or will you break hearts in some rural village?'

Lady Beatrice sighed. 'How cruel you think me. And yet I do not believe men have hearts to break.'

'There speaks a lady who has never been in love.'

She turned with her back to the shifting, restless sea and looked up at him. 'I have been in love, my lord, or thought I was.'

'So what happened?'

She turned back and stood looking out to sea again, so still and quiet that he thought she did not mean to answer him, but at last she said, 'I had just returned from the seminary and my parents were delighted to discover they had a marketable daughter and Mr Blackstone was the highest bidder. But during the period of my engagement, I went to balls and parties during the Season. There I met a young man, handsome and courteous and kind. I was so very much in love with him. I told him I did not want to marry Mr Blackstone and he said I should have nothing to fear. He would marry me himself. All that was required was his parents' permission, for he was dependent on their fortune. He rode off to York where they lived, promising to be back within a month. How I waited! How I dreamt of his return. He had lent me his handkerchief on one occasion at a ball and I slept with it against my cheek. But the days stretched into weeks and he did not come back. The arrangements for my wedding were going ahead. I could not believe he would forget me. Even when my father was leading me up the aisle of St George's, I thought he might come bursting into the church to sweep me away. I learned later that he had married.'

'His name would not be William Purdey, by any chance?' asked Lord Alistair.

She looked up at him in surprise. 'Yes. Do you know him?'

'I met him once when I was visiting friends in Yorkshire. He is about your age and married his bride about the same time as you wed Blackstone. I thought it might be he. Well, I regret to tell you that your lover is a hardened philanderer and causes nothing but grief to his wife and four children.'

'How does he look? Is he as handsome as ever?' She put a hand on his arm and looked appealingly up at his face.

He covered her hand with his own and said quietly, 'He is fat and vulgar. His looks were ruined a long time ago with drinking and womanizing.'

'So,' said Lady Beatrice in a low voice, 'I have wasted years in worry and wondering what happened.'

'He probably was in love with you,' said Lord Alistair. 'Expert philanderers are usually in love with their victims – that is their charm. So you must not go about breaking hearts any more, Lady Beatrice, if this disappointment is what turned you against men. Or flirt with someone like myself, who has no heart to break.'

'And why is that?' she teased. 'Am I not then the only one to have been disappointed in love?'

'No, I have not been disappointed in love, for I have never been in love.' He raised her hand to his lips and smiled down into her eyes.

She smiled back automatically, in the mocking, caressing way she had perfected.

Why he chose that moment to kiss her, he did not know, but one minute he was smiling down at her, quite at his ease, and the next he had jerked her into his arms and crushed his mouth against hers. Her lips caught fire beneath his own and her body was soft and pliant against his, hip against hip, bosom against bosom. Her scent was in his nostrils and he felt quite dizzy.

He released her abruptly and said in a stifled voice, 'You witch!'

'I did not mean . . .' She looked bewildered. She had meant to say that she had never reacted to any man like that before, but his eyes were as cold as ice. She suddenly shivered and with an odd little duck of her head, walked before him into the ballroom.

Lord Alistair remembered he was obliged to take Miss Pym in to supper and hurried to that lady's side.

All Hannah wanted to talk about was the Prince of Wales, what he had said and how he had looked. Lord Alistair sat with her throughout supper and appeared to listen to her while all the time every part of his body was aware of Lady Beatrice, a little way away from him down the long table. She had put a poison in his blood, he thought savagely, which had bound him to her so that although he was not near her or touching her, he could feel her body and taste her lips. And he had thought himself immune.

He interrupted Hannah's paean of praise for the prince by saying abruptly, 'You should reconsider sharing accommodation with Lady Beatrice.'

Hannah looked at him in surprise. 'Why, my lord. I think we suit very well.'

'She is a dangerous and wicked woman. I would like to strangle her.'

'Nonsense, my lord. She is a bitter woman, yes, but surely after the marriage she endured with Blackstone that is understandable. I have found her to have a kind and good heart. Look at her, my lord. All that warmth and beauty to be given away to such an ogre as Sir Geoffrey. Fie! Not if I have anything to say to it!'

Hannah studied him covertly while she ate her food. Something had disturbed him greatly. And then she saw how his eyes kept straying along the table to where Lady Beatrice sat. She was all at once aware of a little glimmer of hope. Lord Alistair's reaction to Lady Beatrice before the ball had been one of calm amusement tinged with disdain. He had not felt powerfully about her at all.

And there was a change in Lady Beatrice. She was partnered at the supper table by an elderly gentleman of staid appearance and yet she was undoubtedly flirting with him, but in a stagy way, as if giving a performance.

Hannah set herself to amuse Lord Alistair by recounting more of her adventures. She wanted to continue to amuse him so that he would continue to call on her and therefore would have ample opportunity of being in Lady Beatrice's company. She succeeded so well in entertaining him that the company, covertly watching her, became even more convinced that this Miss Pym was Someone.

After supper, Lady Beatrice found herself confronted by Sir Geoffrey. Although his eyes sparkled with rage, he appeared to have himself well in check.

'May I suggest,' he said, 'that you owe me an explanation.'

'You are not owed an explanation,' said Lady Beatrice. 'I have found a way to escape and there is nothing you can do about it.'

'You would have come about,' he replied, his eyes roving over her body, from the whiteness of her bosom revealed by the low-cut dress down to her feet, as if he could see through her gown. She instinctively shrank back. 'It is all the fault of that Pym woman,' he said, pasting a smile on his face as he realized they were attracting attention. 'Tell her to walk carefully about the streets of Brighton.'

'Do not dare harm her! She has done nothing. I have merely decided to escape from both you and my parents.'

He moved his face closer to her own. 'Hark 'ee,' he said thickly, 'you will marry me and be glad to by the time I have finished with you.'

She turned on her heel and walked away, leaving him staring after her.

Mrs Cambridge was wondering what to do about Miss Pym. Mrs Cambridge had openly snubbed her, nay, threatened her! All Brighton would now be courting Miss Pym and she, Letitia Cambridge, would be left out in the cold.

Hannah, mindful of her obligations to the dress-maker, was telling all who complimented her on her gown that she bought all her clothes from Monsieur Blanc.

She looked up in surprise as Mrs Cambridge came up to her. 'My dear Miss Pym,' gushed Mrs Cambridge, 'can you ever forgive me? I was so rude to you, but in faith I thought you were someone else.'

'Indeed!' Hannah looked at her frostily.

'Such a terrible, clumsy mistake. Can you forgive me?'

Hannah's odd eyes looked completely colourless as she said, 'I do not know who you thought I was, but I take leave to tell you that no lady should have been subjected to such insult.' She rose quickly from her chair and walked away. Mrs Cambridge stood biting her lip with mortification. Then anger took over. How dare this Miss Pym, if that was her name, snub a leading member of Brighton society! Mrs Cambridge promised herself to get revenge somehow.

Lady Beatrice sought Hannah out. 'Is there somewhere we can sit quietly?' she asked.

'I am surprised you have the time,' said Hannah. 'I would have thought the gentlemen would be queuing up to ask you to dance.'

'Well, they were, but the ladies of Brighton have seen fit to broadcast my heartless reputation, and so I am a wallflower again. Look! The prince is taking his leave, and so that means we too can leave whenever we want.'

'I think I would like to go.' Hannah shook her head ruefully. 'What on earth would all these grand people say if they knew they were courting a mere housekeeper?'

'Ex-housekeeper,' corrected Lady Beatrice. Then she turned a delicate shade of pink. 'Here is Lord Alistair.'

Lord Alistair Munro bowed before them. 'Would either of you ladies care to honour me with a dance?'

'We were on the point of seeking you out to ask you

to escort us home,' said Hannah, 'but I would dearly like to watch you dance with Lady Beatrice.'

To Hannah's surprise there was an awkward silence and then Lady Beatrice said quickly, 'No, let us leave. I am fatigued.'

It was a silent journey the short distance home. Hannah pressed Lord Alistair to take tea with them, and after a little hesitation, he accepted. Benjamin served them efficiently, Hannah was pleased to notice. She wondered how he was getting on with the other servants. She herself had been relieved to find that the presence of a houseful of servants had not fazed her in the least. When tea was served and they were sitting by the fire, Hannah decided to pretend to fall asleep in the hope of dissipating the awkward silence between the couple. She closed her eyes and after a few minutes let out a small snore.

'Poor Miss Pym,' she heard Lady Beatrice say, 'she is quite done up.'

'An eventful evening for her,' came Lord Alistair's voice. 'I must try to dispel this air of embarrassment between us, Lady Beatrice. I should not have kissed you. I crave your forgiveness.'

'Granted, my lord. I have forgot it already.'

There was a long silence. Hannah was about to give up her pretence and open her eyes when she heard Lady Beatrice say, 'I am concerned for Miss Pym.'

'How so?'

'Sir Geoffrey blames her for my freedom. He threatened to harm her.'

'Then I suggest you and Miss Pym leave Brighton immediately.'

'We shall leave soon. I have not told her, for I do not wish to alarm her by what may well turn out to be a choleric and empty threat. More tea?'

'Thank you.'

She leaned across the table and he saw the soft roundness of her breasts and shivered. What would it be like to reach out a hand and caress one of those excellent globes? Then he felt himself becoming angry. She probably knew exactly what she was doing.

'I would tell Benjamin to keep a close watch on Sir Geoffrey,' said Lord Alistair, 'and make sure he does not plan either of you any harm.'

'That is a good idea.' She handed the teacup to him. As he took it from her, his hand brushed against her own. She gave a little cry, and in snatching her hand away, she knocked the cup of tea all over the splendour of his ruffled white cambric shirt.

'I am so sorry,' she said, dabbing furiously at the stain with the edge of the tablecloth.

'It is nothing, nothing at all.' He caught her wrist and held it. They stared at each other in a dawning awareness.

'I am sorry I fell asleep.' Hannah's voice made them both start. Hannah saw the tableau, Lady Beatrice bending over Lord Alistair and he holding her wrist, and wished she had not pretended to wake so soon.

Lord Alistair released Lady Beatrice and she straightened up. 'I am just leaving.' Lord Alistair got to his feet. 'I will have a word with Benjamin on the road out.'

'Why?' asked Hannah, as she was not supposed to have heard their conversation.

'We feel it would be a good idea if your footman kept a close watch on Sir Geoffrey in case . . . in case he plans to make a public scene or something,' said Lady Beatrice hurriedly.

'That is something I feel sure Benjamin would enjoy,' said Hannah drily. 'He is not very domesticated.'

When Lord Alistair had left, Hannah looked at Lady Beatrice curiously. She longed to ask about that kiss. Instead she said, 'A fine gentleman, Lord Alistair. How amazing he has not been snatched up.'

'I would say he is enormously unsnatchable.' Lady Beatrice yawned. 'I must to bed. I have no doubt you will want to swim in the morning at some unearthly hour.'

'Ten o'clock will do,' said Hannah.

'That's what I meant,' said Lady Beatrice and went off to bed.

Hannah walked about the room snuffing the candles. She heard someone enter and turned around. Benjamin stood there. 'Was you wanting anything else, modom?'

'No, Benjamin, that will be all. But stay. How did you come by that splendid livery, not to mention the feathers?'

Benjamin grinned and rattled the dice in his pocket.

'Benjamin, Benjamin,' said Hannah severely. 'One of these days you will go too far and your luck will run out. I fear you will ruin us both, for it is I who will have to bail you out.'

'Won't happen,' said Benjamin confidently. 'The trick to gambling is to know when to stop. Anyways, I'll be too busy watching Sir Geoffrey to gamble.'

'Yes, Lord Alistair told me he wanted him closely watched.' Hannah picked up one remaining candle in its stick to light her way to bed. 'Be careful, Benjamin. He may seem a figure of fun, a blustering noisy idiot, but I fear he is also evil and dangerous.'

'Pooh!' said Benjamin, and ignoring his mistress's severe remark that good footmen did not pooh, he left the drawing-room and ran lightly down the stairs.

6

A man who is not afraid of the sea will soon be drownded, he said, for he will be going out on a day he shouldn't. But we do be afraid of the sea, and we do only be drownded now and again.

J.M. Synge

Lady Beatrice's lady's maid left the very next day. The servants had been told to find new posts as soon as possible, but Lady Beatrice had not expected them to be so quick off the mark. But she quickly consoled herself with the thought that she would soon have to live without a retinue of servants.

The news of her rapidly dwindling staff reached the interested ears of Sir Geoffrey Handford and his mother. Although Mrs Hanford had done much to caution her son against abducting Lady Beatrice and forcing her to marry him, her only reason was that Miss Pym might call on the Prince of Wales to intercede. She had, however, urged her son to bribe one of the housemaids in Lady Beatrice's establishment to report on her comings and goings. While she was discussing the matter with Sir Geoffrey, a footman entered to tell them both the interesting news that the Prince of Wales had left Brighton that very day for London and most of society was following him to the metropolis.

'Now we have a different scene,' said Sir Geoffrey, rubbing his hands.

'But you still must be careful,' warned his mother. 'You can hardly drag her out of her house or accost her in the street without occasioning a scandal.'

'Let's have that housemaid – what's her name – over here to report,' said Sir Geoffrey. 'I'll send someone to fetch her.'

Benjamin, leaning against the railings outside Lady Beatrice's mansion and picking his teeth, saw a footman in Sir Geoffrey's livery scuttling down the area steps. He waited, interested. After ten minutes the footman emerged followed by Josephine, one of the housemaids, and they made their way off together along the street. Benjamin followed them at a discreet distance.

He noticed that Josephine was not taken to the servants' entrance but shown in at the front door.

He decided to wait.

'Well?' demanded Sir Geoffrey when Josephine was ushered in.

Josephine bobbed a curtsy. 'Her ladyship has been taking walks with that Miss Pym and she bathes in the sea most mornings.'

'Lord Alistair Munro appeared to be paying her particular attention at the ball,' said Mrs Handford. 'Has he been calling?'

'Not since the ball, madame,' said Josephine. 'No gentleman callers, and no ladies neither. Day after the ball, a lot of people called then, but were told that neither Miss Pym nor my lady were receiving company, and so they were both left quiet.'

Sir Geoffrey surveyed the housemaid for a long moment. 'When they go bathing, do they take a servant with them?'

'Just that footman o' Miss Pym's.'

'Can he swim?'

'No, sir. He says that folks who go in the sea must be mad. He's forever trying to stop his mistress from going in, but she will have none o' it.'

'Very well, Josephine. You are a good girl.' He took out several coins and passed them over.

Josephine emerged alone from the house and Benjamin let her go a little way and then caught up with her and fell into step beside her. 'What are you following me for?' demanded Josephine.

'I'm not following you, you silly wench,' said Benjamin. 'Where were you anyways?'

'Out looking for a new post, if you must know,' said Josephine pertly. 'Mistress says as how we could take time off to find new places.'

Benjamin regarded her thoughtfully. She was a

buxom girl with a turned-up nose and a wide mouth and a quantity of copper curls under a jaunty cap. 'You could say as how you was going to see a new employer and take a walk with me,' said Benjamin.

'Oh, go on.'

'You're a pretty lass and it seems a shame you should spend all your time dusting and cleaning.'

Josephine threw him a flirtatious look. 'What had you in mind?'

'We could take a walk along the shore, see the nobs.'

'Won't that mistress o' yourn be in the sea as usual?'

'She don't really need me,' said Benjamin, conscious that his instructions were to take as much free time as he wanted so long as he kept an eye on Sir Geoffrey.

'I'll go,' said Josephine. 'But only for a little, mind.'

Benjamin squeezed her around the waist and she shrieked with laughter and pushed him away in mock horror.

Hannah was therefore told by her footman that the maid Josephine had called at Sir Geoffrey's and was no doubt being paid to keep an eye on them.

'I'll turn the hussy off now,' said Lady Beatrice, who had been listening.

'No, don't do that,' said Benjamin. 'I have persuaded her to go out walking with me tomorrow morning. If we challenge her with it now, she will only say as how she was looking for new employ and Sir Geoffrey would no doubt say so as well. As to the rest of the day, ladies, if I'm to follow Sir Geoffrey, I must ha' some sort o' disguise.'

'I have a trunk of my late husband's clothes which were brought down to Brighton by mistake,' said Lady Beatrice. 'In fact, I thought I had given away all his stuff. Tell the butler to show you where it is, and take what you need, Benjamin. Dressed finely as a gentleman and with your hair unpowdered would be a better disguise that creeping about Brighton under a set of false whiskers.'

The peacock that was Benjamin was delighted. He appeared before them later attired in a blue swallow-tail coat, striped waistcoat, canary-yellow pantaloons, and Hessian boots. The coat was padded on the shoulders and chest. Lady Beatrice shuddered. 'I had forgot how awful my husband's taste was,' she said.

But Benjamin, highly pleased with himself, went off to hunt down Sir Geoffrey. That gentleman emerged late in the afternoon with his mother. They made various calls. In the evening, Sir Geoffrey went out alone. Benjamin followed him to a tavern where Sir Geoffrey sat and drank and bragged with a group of noisy acquaintances, but although Benjamin listened as hard as he could, not once did he hear Lady Beatrice's name mentioned, or see Sir Geoffrey seek out anyone who might do her harm.

Lady Beatrice and Hannah walked out for their usual morning's swim the next day, a footman behind them carrying their bathing dresses and towels. He was instructed to leave them on the beach and return in a half-hour to collect their wet things.

The weather was blustery but not too cold. They were the only ladies on the beach. The other members of their sex did not venture into the water unless the day was sunny and the sea calm.

Benjamin, with Josephine on his arm, came strolling towards the beach where he could keep an eye on Hannah. 'Where was you earlier?' demanded Benjamin. 'I thought you wasn't coming.'

'Looking for that job,' said Josephine with a toss of her curls.

'With Sir Geoffrey Handford?'

Josephine pulled her arm away. 'And what if I was?'

'Nothing against it,' said Benjamin with a grin. 'But don't it seem odd, you trying to get into a household where the master plans to harm Lady Beatrice?'

Josephine gave a superior titter. 'That's what you think. He's mad about her.'

Benjamin put an arm about the maid's shoulders. 'Come on, now,' he said with an indulgent laugh. 'You don't know nothing.'

'Suit yourself!' said Josephine, looking sulky.

Benjamin drew a guinea from his pocket and held it up so that the gold winked in the pale sunlight. 'Tell you what,' he said, 'you can have this to buy silk ribbons if you tell me what's afoot.'

Josephine's eyes gleamed. She reached for the gold but he laughed and held it high above his head. 'Come on, now, pretty. Out with it.'

'Oh, all right,' said Josephine. 'But you mustn't tell anyone.'

Benjamin solemnly crossed his heart.

'I went there this morning,' said Josephine, 'for he wanted to know the exact time she was going in the sea. I told him, but I listened at the door when he thought I'd left. He was speaking to that valet of his ... Jackson. Seems Jackson's hired some men to pluck her out of the sea, put her in a boat, and take her to where Sir Geoffrey can talk to her and tell her how much he loves her. If we stand here, we can watch.'

Benjamin's mind raced. He was not even aware of Josephine snatching the gold coin from him. He did not believe Sir Geoffrey wanted a romantic meeting. He wanted to abduct Lady Beatrice again, and this time constrain her by force to marry him. And what of Miss Pym? He would want her out of the way.

Benjamin sprinted down to the water's edge and began to run up and down like a barking terrier, calling to Hannah. But the wind whipped his words away.

He looked this way and that for help. And then he saw, far along the beach, Lord Alistair Munro with his valet, preparing for *his* morning swim.

Hannah Pym was in seventh heaven. She had discovered that if she paddled her arms energetically enough and took her feet off the bottom and thrashed them about, she could keep afloat for a few minutes. When she rested for a moment, she saw with surprise that a rowing-boat with three men in it was lying a little way out, the men resting on the oars.

She frowned and began to make her way towards Lady Beatrice. They had better go in so as to avoid the vulgar gaze of these men, who obviously did not know the etiquette of bathing in Brighton, which was that no man should be seen near the ladies' bathing machines. She then saw to her amazement that her own bathing machine had retreated back up the beach, horse and all. Lady Beatrice's bathing machine was still there, but of her bathing attendant there was no sign.

'Beatrice!' shouted Hannah in sudden terror.

And then someone or something grabbed at her ankles and she felt herself being pulled down under the water.

Benjamin, back on the shore after having alerted Lord Alistair, saw her disappear. All his terror of the ocean fled. Fully clothed, he waded into the sea. A man had surfaced and had caught Lady Beatrice and was swimming out towards the boat with her, but Benjamin's fears were all for his mistress. He ploughed doggedly on until the waves were slapping his face. Hannah suddenly surfaced in front of him and he seized her. She was gasping and spluttering, but very much alive. She clung desperately to Benjamin crying, 'Someone tried to drown me. Lady Beatrice . . .'

Benjamin pulled her towards the shore and with a strong arm around her waist dragged her to the safety of the beach, where he laid her down on the shingle. Hannah turned on her side and was desperately sick.

Lord Alistair was swimming as hard as he could towards Lady Beatrice and her abductor. He knew he had to get to them before they reached the boat. One final powerful stroke brought him up to them. The man let Lady Beatrice go and Lord Alistair raised his fist and struck the man a powerful savage blow on the head, then he dived and caught Lady Beatrice and dragged her to the surface. She began to struggle weakly but she was exhausted, having struggled so long with her captor. 'It is I, Munro,' he shouted. 'Put your arms around my neck and hold tightly and I will get you in.'

With a feeling of sheer gladness, Hannah saw Lord Alistair swimming strongly for the shore with Lady Beatrice. The man who had tried to abduct her was being pulled aboard the boat by the other men and then they rowed swiftly away.

Lord Alistair had meant to hand Lady Beatrice into the care of the bathing attendant, but when he reached the machine, there was no one there. He pushed Lady Beatrice forward and up the steps and then followed her up. In the salty darkness of the bathing machine, he picked up a large fleecy towel and wrapped it around her. 'You had better get dried as quickly as possible,' he said.

Lady Beatrice sat down suddenly on the bench at the back of the box. Her teeth were chattering and her face was white. Stark naked, Lord Alistair stood over her and looked down at her with concern. 'Where is your maid?' he demanded.

'Left me,' said Lady Beatrice. 'Miss Pym? Where is Miss Pym?'

'I shall find out for you.'

She held out her hand and said simply, 'Thank you, my lord.'

He bowed from the waist and courteously kissed her hand.

Lady Beatrice began to laugh weakly. 'My lord, you are as naked as the day you were born.' She stood up. 'Leave me and I will dry and change.'

He half turned away from her. Her gown was plastered to her body and her hair was like seaweed and her face was as white as milk and yet he suddenly thought he had never seen anything so beautiful in the whole of his life. He wrapped his arms around her and kissed her salty, quivering lips, holding her tightly against his naked body. Then, with a stifled exclamation, he released her, wrenched open the door of the bathing machine, and unhitched the reins of the horse, which were looped over a hook at the side of the door. 'Walk forward,' he cried.

The obedient horse began to turn in the sea and placidly make its way to its station on the beach. He was relieved to see Hannah standing there, supported by Benjamin. It was only when Hannah blushed and turned her head away that he realized what a spectacle he was making of himself, driving a lady's bathing machine without a stitch on.

His valet came running up and leaped up on the platform and shrouded his master in towels.

The sufferers gathered together in Lady Beatrice's drawing-room two hours later. Hannah reflected that she had never seen either Lady Beatrice or Lord Alistair so grandly dressed or looking so haughty and remote. She wondered just what had happened in that bathing machine.

'The facts as we have them are this,' said Hannah. 'The maid, Josephine, has disappeared for good. All her belongings are gone, too. The bathing attendants, that is mine and Lady Beatrice's, confess freely that they were heavily bribed to make themselves scarce because they were told a gentleman wanted to keep a romantic assignment in the sea. Both said such a thing had happened before. The authorities are searching for those men but evidently with little hope of finding them. Sir Geoffrey was out walking with his mother, nowhere near the beach. He is complaining bitterly that Lady Beatrice, not content with humiliating him with breaking off the engagement, is hell-bent on humiliating him further by claiming he had paid ruffians to abduct her and that it has nothing to do with him. Asked about his valet, he says his valet is on holiday. What are we to do?'

'I could call him out,' said Lord Alistair.

'A duel? No, that would never do,' said Lady Beatrice. 'I could not bear the scandal.'

He looked at her frostily. 'There is one fact you may have overlooked, Lady Beatrice. Some interested spectators noticed me entering your bathing box naked. There is already scandal, and to lay such a scandal, I fear you must marry me.'

There was a long silence. Hannah looked at the couple hopefully. Lady Beatrice was sitting on a backless sofa. She was wearing a green-and-gold-striped gown which showed her splendid figure to advantage. She was so still that the emerald brooch at the neck of her gown glowed with an unwinking dull green fire.

Then she said in a flat voice, 'You have done enough, my lord. There is no need for you to sacrifice yourself on the altar of marriage.'

'I think there is every need.' He strode to the window and looked out at the sea, his well-tailored back to her.

Hannah signalled to Benjamin and both quietly left the room. Hannah went only as far as the outside of the door. She turned and leaned her ear against the panels. Benjamin, already halfway down the stairs, saw her and darted back to join her and put his ear to the door as well.

'It's awfully quiet in there,' he whispered.

'Shhh!' said Hannah fiercely.

'My lord,' said Lady Beatrice, 'I know you wish to save my reputation, but reputation in my present circumstances no longer concerns me. I shall live quietly in the countryside somewhere with Miss Pym.'

'Then have a thought to Miss Pym! Your damaged reputation might taint hers.'

'By the end of the week, Brighton will have found something else to talk about. The circumstances were unusual. You saved me, my lord. Everyone knows that. Apart from a few scurrilous tongues, the rest will only admire you. I shall never marry again. And you, my lord, must never feel constrained to marry anyone out of duty.'

There was a long silence. Each was obscurely hoping that the other would make some move, show some sign of warmth, but Lady Beatrice was frightened of the effect he had on her senses. She had at long last gained freedom. If she gave in to him, she would never know freedom again. He would possess her mind and feelings and thoughts. Lord Alistair thought she had deliberately bewitched him, as she had bewitched so many. He was damned if he would let her know his proposal was prompted by other than duty.

'As you will,' he said indifferently.

Lady Beatrice felt a lump rise in her throat. 'Where on earth is Miss Pym?' she demanded.

Hannah opened the door and went in. 'I had to fetch something,' she said mendaciously.

'I bid you good day,' said Lord Alistair. 'You will no doubt be much occupied during the remainder of your stay in Brighton. Perhaps we may meet again one day.'

'Perhaps,' said Lady Beatrice, forcing a smile.

Hannah looked at him miserably. Then she thought of something. As he was making for the door, she said, 'I am sad that we can no longer count on your protection.'

He stopped and stood frowning. 'After today's episode, I doubt if Sir Geoffrey will ever dare to try anything again.'

'Oh, I think he will,' said Hannah, growing more cheerful. 'I should think this set-back will make him more than ever determined to succeed.'

With something curiously approaching relief, Lord Alistair said slowly, 'In that case, perhaps I should call on you. How long do you plan to remain here?'

Hannah looked inquiringly at Lady Beatrice. 'Only another week,' she said, 'if that suits you, Miss Pym. Then I must return to London and sell what effects I can before my parents sell the house.'

'That will be quite all right,' said Hannah, although the idea of returning to London with the dashing Lady Beatrice did not suit her at all. Always in her mind's eye was the picture of her little apartment in South Audley Street and of Sir George Clarence sitting on the other side of the tea-table listening to her recount her adventures.

'Perhaps,' said Hannah firmly, 'it might be a good idea if you called on us during the coming week, Lord Alistair. I should feel so uneasy and worried were your protection removed from us.'

'I shall be glad to call on you,' he said. He swept them a low bow and then he was gone. Lady Beatrice buried her face in her hands and suddenly began to cry. Hannah fussed over her, saying she was over-wrought, saying she must rest after her ordeal. But Lady Beatrice was crying over her past behaviour, over all the men she had so cruelly led on and then rejected. She wondered whether any of them had felt so desolate as she did now. She wanted Lord Alistair to admire her, to love her, to cherish her, and she felt he never would. The ice around her heart had melted and all she could feel was pain.

* * *

Mrs Handford's bulldog face was a muddy colour. 'Are you mad, Geoffrey?' she demanded, not for the first time. 'Let us leave Brighton and leave Lady Beatrice alone. What if just one of those villains that Jackson hired had been caught and decided to talk. Think of the scandal! You could never hope for a title, and that very knighthood you now seem to hold so cheap would be taken from you.'

'I covered my tracks,' he growled. 'Did I not send Jackson off on leave directly he had set the matter up?'

'But that maid, Josephine. What if she were found?'

'She won't be,' he said tersely. 'I told her what would happen to her if she opened her mouth. Why must the silly wench go blabbing to that footman of Miss Pym's?'

'Because we did not think she would go about listening at doors and that is what she must have done; else why would that footman have been alerted in time to call Lord Alistair to the rescue? Let the matter drop, my son. Lady Beatrice is not for you.'

'I want her,' he said passionately. 'Cannot you realize that? And I mean to have her. I am rich. Men can be bribed, and yes, even justices, should things go wrong.'

'What of Lord Alistair Munro? He has powerful friends, and among those powerful friends is the Prince of Wales. It was said that Lord Alistair was naked in her bathing box!'

Sir Geoffrey's face darkened. 'I'll find some discreet way to put him out of commission.'

His mother shrank back in her chair. She was

beginning to fear for her son's sanity and cursed Lady Beatrice from the bottom of her heart.

With the departure of the Prince of Wales and his entourage from Brighton, gossip about Miss Pym quickly died. She had not been invited to the Marine Pavilion, she had not followed him to London, there was much more exciting gossip about the prince's current mistress, Lady Jersey, and so people no longer turned to stare when she went past. Monsieur Blanc refused to talk about Miss Pym. The ball gown had been returned to him in perfect condition and the terrible footman had not betrayed the secret of the dressmaker's nationality, and so Monsieur Blanc was anxious to distance himself from a lady whose footman had the power to ruin him.

Only Letitia Cambridge was still interested in Miss Pym's comings and goings, although she did not tell her friends this. She did, however, call on Mrs Handford and warmly pressed that lady's hand and sympathized with her over her 'poor' son's broken engagement. 'He is not to be blamed,' said Mrs Cambridge. 'Neither is Lady Beatrice. The fault, I am convinced, lies with that female, Miss Pym. Mark my words, she has poisoned Lady Beatrice's mind against Sir Geoffrey.'

And forgetting that Lady Beatrice had never wanted to marry her beloved son, Mrs Handford listened eagerly, for surely it was Miss Pym who had persuaded Lady Beatrice to disobey her parents.

'All poor Geoffrey wants,' said Mrs Handford, 'is an opportunity to see Lady Beatrice alone. You must admit, Mrs Cambridge, he is vastly handsome, and I am sure he would succeed in wooing her were he allowed a few moments in private with her. And what of Lord Alistair Munro? Naked in her bathing box!'

'As always,' said Mrs Cambridge sourly, 'Lord Alistair has the ear of the influential, and so there is no scandal. Instead he is hailed as a hero for having rescued her. But you have nothing to fear, dear Mrs Handford. Everyone knows Lord Alistair to be a confirmed bachelor.'

'Nonetheless,' said Mrs Hanford uneasily, 'why does he remain in Brighton with the prince gone?'

Mrs Cambridge patted one of Mrs Handford's fat be-ringed hands. 'He never did follow the prince. I am anxious to help you in any way I can.'

Mrs Handford did not find this behaviour at all strange, although she should have, considering the fact that Mrs Cambridge had gone out of her way in the past to cut the Handfords socially. 'If only you could,' she said.

'I could watch them,' said Mrs Cambridge eagerly, 'and let you know when Lady Beatrice is alone, and then you could tell Sir Geoffrey to make his call.'

'We would be most indebted to you,' said Mrs Handford warmly. She knew her son had already tried to find another servant in Lady Beatrice's household to give him information, but without success.

Mrs Cambridge threw herself into her new role of spy with enthusiasm. She wore a dark gown and pelisse and a heavy veil for the purpose of following

Miss Pym and Lady Beatrice. After one exhausting day, she reflected sourly that the couple seemed to be inseparable. Not only that, but they were followed everywhere by that footman of Miss Pym's.

But on the second day, she had better luck. In the afternoon, Hannah emerged alone. The veiled figure that was Mrs Cambridge, followed by her veiled maid, set off in pursuit. Hannah stopped for a moment to look out to sea. She had not been bathing since her adventure. She wondered if she would ever have the courage to go into the sea again. She was once more lashed into her stays and a little piece of whalebone had worked itself loose from the cloth and was digging painfully into the soft flesh under her armpit. She glanced back and noticed two heavily veiled women watching her. They looked odd against the background of the green-and-blue sea, two still, mourning figures with noisy sea-gulls wheeling about them.

Hannah turned away and walked on. She was determined to stay away as long as possible. Benjamin had asked for the afternoon off, but Hannah did not mind being on her own. Lady Beatrice was left at home and, with any luck, thought Hannah, Lord Alistair might call, and something might come of that.

Mrs Cambridge paused and took out a prepared letter and gave it to her maid. 'Run with that to Sir Geoffrey Handford,' she ordered. The letter told Sir Geoffrey that he might find Lady Beatrice alone if he called immediately. Now, thought Mrs Cambridge, to try to keep that Pym woman from returning home too soon.

Hannah sat gloomily at the table by the window of the pastry cook's where she had sat before with Lord Alistair and Lady Beatrice. She felt very flat and depressed, but glad for the first time that Lady Beatrice was not with her. Being with Lady Beatrice, reflected Hannah, was rather like becoming invisible. Lady Beatrice was so very beautiful that all stared at her and no one seemed to notice plain Miss Pym at her side, particularly now that Miss Pym was no longer a subject of gossip. Hannah thought of entertaining Sir George Clarence to tea. She could see him in her mind's eye, his silver hair, his piercing blue eyes, but those blue eyes, instead of resting on *her*, were resting with admiration on Lady Beatrice's beautiful face.

I must get rid of her, thought Hannah. Why did I ever ask her to live with me? I have not finished my journeys. I have not seen England. She herself, she knew, could learn to become content with a quiet life in some English village. But what of Lady Beatrice? Surely she would soon become restless and bored. Besides, the rent on the flat in South Audley Street had been paid for a year. It was a very fashionable address, but continuing to live there with Lady Beatrice meant putting Lady Beatrice next to Sir George, who lived hard by. Not that Lady Beatrice would surely be interested in a retired diplomat in his fifties. But could he possibly remain uninterested in her?

There must be some way to throw Lady Beatrice and Lord Alistair together.

A shadow fell across her and she looked up. A veiled woman was standing there. She threw back her veil and Hannah immediately recognized Mrs Cambridge.

'Do not be angry,' said Mrs Cambridge. 'I desire to speak to you.'

'About what?' demanded Hannah suspiciously.

'You must forgive me for my appalling behaviour, but you see, I was so convinced that you had deliberately set out to make fools of us all.'

'Pray be seated.' Hannah indicated a chair opposite. She felt somewhat mollified. After all, it was Benjamin's lie to the dressmaker which had started all the fuss.

'I confess,' said Hannah, after ordering tea for Mrs Cambridge, 'that I was very angry indeed, but now, on cooler reflection, I can understand why you became so exercised on the matter.'

'We shall put it behind us,' said Mrs Cambridge, 'and talk of other things. How long do you and Lady Beatrice intend to remain in Brighton?'

'About a week,' said Hannah, although her mind was beginning to race. Why should Mrs Cambridge be interested in the length of their stay? The most normal thing to have asked was all about the attempted abduction of Lady Beatrice.

'Indeed. Brighton will be sorry to lose you. How do you intend to travel? I believe you came on the stage. How original.'

Hannah glanced at Mrs Cambridge's heavy veil, which was now hanging down about her shoulders, pulled back over her hat to reveal her face. She remembered the two heavily veiled women standing a little way away from her. Mrs Cambridge and her maid?

'Do you know Sir Geoffrey Handford?' asked Hannah, ignoring the last question.

Mrs Cambridge affected surprise. 'Slightly,' she said dismissively. 'Have you known Lady Beatrice long?'

'Only since I came to Brighton,' replied Hannah, thinking suddenly that she had left Lady Beatrice alone apart from the remaining servants. And where was Mrs Cambridge's maid?

'Where is your maid?' asked Hannah.

'What has that got to do with how long you have known Lady Beatrice?' countered Mrs Cambridge.

'Nothing,' said Hannah, eyeing her. 'Again, I ask, where is your maid?'

'I don't know,' said Mrs Cambridge pettishly. 'Oh, I remember, I sent her to match silks for me.'

'I am curious. I also wonder why you are both so heavily veiled. I saw you and your maid a little way away from me on the promenade,' said Hannah.

'It is the rough wind.' Mrs Cambridge began to look even more uneasy. 'So rough and blustery and so bad for the complexion.'

Hannah got to her feet. 'I really must go,' she said abruptly, and strode out of the pastry cook's, leaving an infuriated Mrs Cambridge to pay the bill.

She did not trust Mrs Cambridge. Alert to possible danger on all sides, Hannah felt sure that Mrs Cambridge had been spying on her. She was now very worried that she had left Lady Beatrice alone.

* * *

Lady Beatrice was at that moment confronting Sir Geoffrey Handford. He had pushed his way past her servants, who obviously did not know what to do to restrain him.

'You may think you have had the better of me, madam,' raged Sir Geoffrey, 'but you shall pay for it.'

'With my life?' demanded Lady Beatrice.

He stopped in mid-tirade and looked at her with his mouth open.

'I am not stupid, Sir Geoffrey, and know that you hired those ruffians to abduct me. You cannot do anything to me now with all my servants listening at the door.'

He began to pace up and down. He suddenly regretted his impetuousness. The minute he had received that note from Mrs Cambridge's maid, he had come dashing round. His desire for her had not waned in the least. Rather, it had become an obsession.

He looked at her in baffled fury.

'And now you may take your leave.' Lady Beatrice looked at him in contempt. 'And do not try to harm me again, Sir Geoffrey, or it will be the worse for you.'

'And who will stop me?' he jeered. 'The few servants you have left? One faded spinster and her cheeky footman?'

'No, but I will stop you,' said a quiet voice from the doorway.

Sir Geoffrey wheeled round. Lord Alistair Munro stood there, tall and elegant as ever.

'So she has caught you in her wiles, like every other

poor fool that has had anything to do with her,' shouted Sir Geoffrey, beside himself with rage and jealousy. 'She plays with us all like a cat plays with a mouse. Well, more fool you, Munro. Take her, and be damned to you!'

He thrust his way past Lord Alistair and past the gaping servants and stormed out of the house.

There was a long silence. The servants retreated to go about their duties, talking in excited whispers.

'Thank you,' said Lady Beatrice at last. 'Thank you again. Your arrival was most timely.'

'I am grateful to be of service.' He swept her a low bow.

'Pray be seated, my lord,' said Lady Beatrice, 'and I will get you some refreshment. Wine? We have a very good claret.'

He looked at her thoughtfully. She was wearing a blue muslin gown, cunningly cut and shaped to her handsome figure. Her hair was dressed high on her head but one black curl had been allowed to fall on the whiteness of her shoulder. He felt a surge of desire and was impatient with himself. That churl, Handford, had the right of it. Lady Beatrice was a witch.

'I have calls to make,' he said. 'I see Miss Pym is not here. I am disappointed. A most entertaining lady.'

Lady Beatrice suddenly felt jealous of the absent Hannah. 'Then I shall not detain you, my lord.'

He bowed again, and backed into Hannah, who had come flying up the stairs.

'My lord!' cried Hannah. 'I am so very glad to see you. I was detained by Mrs Cambridge and had the maddest idea she was doing it deliberately.'

'That might have been the case,' said Lord Alistair. 'Handford did call, but left in a fury.'

'Because you were here?'

'Yes,' put in Lady Beatrice, 'most certainly because Lord Alistair arrived.'

'But you cannot leave now!' said Hannah to Lord Alistair. 'You must stay and take a dish of tea with us.'

To Lady Beatrice's mortification, Lord Alistair smiled and said he would be delighted.

'I thought you had urgent calls to make,' snapped Lady Beatrice.

He smiled at her lazily. 'None that take precedence over tea with Miss Pym.'

Hannah watched the couple covertly all the while she was telling them about the veiled Mrs Cambridge who had accosted her at the pastry cook's. Lady Beatrice handed Lord Alistair a plate of cakes. His hand inadvertently brushed against her own and Lady Beatrice's own hand shook.

'There is no doubt,' said Lord Alistair when Hannah had finished talking, 'that Handford has people watching you. You must leave Brighton as soon as possible.'

'He might pursue us,' said Hannah anxiously.

'In that case, may I offer you my escort?'

'Gladly,' said Hannah quickly, before Lady Beatrice could speak.

'In that case, I would suggest we leave tomorrow evening, at, say, six o'clock.'

'Splendid!' Hannah clapped her hands.

Lady Beatrice said in a voice that sounded pettish

to her own ears, 'But I have much to arrange. The servants . . .'

'The servants, the few that are left, can be sent to London in the morning,' said Hannah eagerly. 'I am very good at organizing things, Lady Beatrice. Do, I beg of you, let me arrange all.'

Lady Beatrice frowned. She found the very presence of Lord Alistair made her heart ache. He held her in contempt. He had not considered her important enough to put before his other calls and yet he had stayed for Miss Pym. But to protest would mean explaining why, and that she could not possibly do.

And so it was all settled. Lord Alistair would call for them in his travelling carriage at six o'clock the following evening.

After he had left and Hannah had gone off to arrange the servants' affairs, Lady Beatrice rested her head on her hand and for the first time thought bleakly of the future. She would be trapped for life in some quaint English village with the domineering Miss Pym. Miss Pym would no doubt be supremely happy, but what of herself?

7

Love is like the measles, we all have to go through it.

Jerome K. Jerome

Hannah, her arrangements completed, told Benjamin that evening that she wished to take the air and he was to accompany her. Benjamin looked startled, for the rain was rattling against the shutters and a gale howled mournfully in from the sea.

'The almanac says the weather is going to be fine tomorrow, modom,' said Benjamin in injured tones. 'Why not wait until then?'

'When will you ever learn to obey an order?' shouted Hannah, and Lady Beatrice looked up from the book she was reading in surprise.

Benjamin, injured, stalked off like an offended cat

to get his coat and hat. Hannah, already dressed to go out, made for the door. 'I have arranged everything for your removal to London,' said Hannah, turning on the threshold. 'The servants will go ahead first thing in the morning, Lady Beatrice.'

'Thank you,' said Lady Beatrice in a tired voice. 'You are indefatigable, Miss Pym.'

'I have great energy,' said Hannah. 'Do not worry. We shall not be bored in our little village, whichever one we choose. I have great schemes. It has always been my desire to help Fallen Women, and then there are clothes to be made for the poor, and oh, so many things.' She walked out and left Lady Beatrice to her gloomy thoughts.

It was all very well to want to atone for a rather selfish and dissolute past, thought Lady Beatrice miserably, but somehow the thought of doing good works under the eagle eye of Hannah Pym was very lowering. She could picture herself stitching away busily by candle-light in some poky cottage, occasionally reviving the tedium of the long winter evenings by reading in the social columns how London's most eligible bachelor, Lord Alistair Munro, was charming society during the Little Season. She would have been amazed had she but known that Hannah had set out deliberately to give her a dreary picture of their life together. It was not the idea of good works that was so depressing, thought Lady Beatrice, but the idea of being bossed around for the rest of her life by Miss Hannah Pym.

Meanwhile, Hannah strode along the beach, her boots crunching in the shingle, followed by Benjamin.

A particularly large wave washed over Benjamin's feet and he cursed and jumped back.

'Tide's coming in,' he shouted against the wind.

'We must find somewhere where we can talk,' said Hannah, turning to face him. 'There is much to be planned.'

'I know a nice warm tavern,' said Benjamin hopefully. 'You'll catch your death being out on a night like this.'

The tavern to which Benjamin led Hannah was a modest one. The coffee room served as the dining-room, but dinner had been served long ago and it was empty save for a prim gentleman in the corner smoking a long clay pipe and reading the newspapers.

'You may sit down with me, Benjamin,' said Hannah. Benjamin gratefully sank down in a chair next to her. Hannah ordered ratafia for herself and beer for Benjamin and then regarded him thoughtfully.

'I do not want to spend the rest of my life with Lady Beatrice,' she said. 'I feel she would become bossy and domineering.'

Benjamin put a hand up to his mouth to hide a smile.

'I feel that she may be enamoured of Lord Alistair Munro.'

'Don't think they care for each other meself,' said Benjamin, burying his nose in his tankard.

'I think you are wrong,' said Hannah. 'Besides, he was naked in her bathing box.' Hannah coloured faintly. 'It is only fitting they should wed. He is, I believe, immensely rich. 'Twould be all that is suitable, and even her greedy parents would come round.'

'Mayhap something will happen on the road to London,' said Benjamin comfortably. 'I went around to talk to Lord Alistair's coachman. Bang-up rig, he's got. Fifteen-mile-an-hour nags and the best-sprung travelling carriage you ever did see. Better'n a nasty smelly old stage anydays. Brought down from London a few days ago.'

'I do not think we shall be travelling with Lord Alistair.'

'But you said . . .'

'I didn't say anything, Benjamin. I think we should go quietly ourselves on the stage. There is one that leaves Brighton at six.'

'But, modom!' wailed Benjamin in protest.

'Listen! Propinquity is the answer. Without us, they will be forced to travel together, to talk to each other, to get to know each other better.'

'Could not they do that in London?' protested Benjamin, who still hoped to be able to journey in Lord Alistair's splendid travelling carriage.

'No, no. They will go their separate ways. Cast off by her parents and living with me will put Lady Beatrice effectively out of society and she will have no chance to see him again. We must hope and pray. Benjamin. Let us go to the booking-office now.'

A particularly vicious gust of wind drove rain against the windows of the coffee room. Benjamin shivered. 'I'll go first thing in the morning, modom.'

'Very well.' Hannah looked reluctant. 'Have your things packed and ready. Lady Beatrice does not rise until late. We will take our baggage to the Ship and will simply leave the house during the afternoon and then have a letter delivered to Lady Beatrice at ten minutes to six, saying she must go ahead without us.'

They finished their drinks and walked back together through the windy rain-swept streets under the swinging oil lamps.

Mrs Cambridge was on a diet. Although plumpness was in fashion, fat was not, and she had suddenly begun to grow rounder and rounder. Layers of fat had crept up her back, where it hung in ugly creases, and her diamond choker would need to be altered to fit her neck. Mrs Cambridge sighed. She would never have believed that her very neck could put on weight.

She rose very early, ate a beefsteak and washed it down with a pint of old port and set out to take her morning's constitutional along the beach. She did not take a maid or a footman, for such villains as Brighton possessed were still sleeping off the dissipations of the night and the streets were empty.

Mrs Cambridge was approaching the Ship Inn and telling herself that a plate of shrimps could hardly be counted as *eating*, when she saw the tall figure of Benjamin going towards the coaching booking-office. She waited around a corner until she saw him emerge and then entered the booking-office herself. She asked about fares to various places and then demanded idly, 'I thought I recognized Miss Pym's footman. Is she taking the stage? We are very dear friends and I might be persuaded to go with her.'

The clerk said that the footman had booked tickets on the London stage, which was to depart at six o'clock that very evening.

'Perhaps I should consult her first,' said Mrs Cambridge airily and took her leave.

So, thought Mrs Cambridge, Sir Geoffrey will be most interested in this piece of news. For Mrs Cambridge assumed that Lady Beatrice would be travelling with Miss Pym. To celebrate her successful bit of spying, she entered the Ship and ordered those shrimps.

It was much later in the morning when she reached Sir Geoffrey's, for an obstacle in the shape of a pastry cook's had loomed in her path and she felt she deserved some cakes after all her exertions. Sir Geoffrey listened to her closely. Mrs Handford said, with an air of relief, 'She is beyond your reach now, Geoffrey. You cannot descend on her in London and make jealous scenes.'

He rounded on his mother furiously – both mother and son having forgotten the very presence of Letitia Cambridge – and said, 'She will not reach London.'

'You were lucky last time,' said Mrs Handford urgently. 'This time, Miss Pym will shout for the constable.'

'She won't get a chance,' jeered Sir Geoffrey. 'High time someone stopped that interfering busybody's mouth.'

Mrs Cambridge shrank back in her chair. Like most ladies of her class, she was only dimly aware of the brutish side of the gentlemen she met in drawing-rooms or balls. Women, although damned as the inferior sex, benefited in a way by being treated like delicate children. No uncouth words or thoughts were revealed to them, and they were rarely subjected to any shocking lusts, it being tacitly understood that gentlemen who required such diversions took their pleasures outside the home.

She rose to leave. Her stomach felt queasy and her conscience, never much exercised, nonetheless was giving her several painful jabs.

Neither mother nor son appeared aware of her going. Mrs Cambridge stood outside the house, irresolute. She felt she ought to warn Lady Beatrice. But, on the other hand, perhaps she was reading too much into Sir Geoffrey's remarks about stopping Miss Pym's mouth.

She trailed off home and ate a light luncheon of soup, grilled sole and potatoes and tartlets, all washed down with a bottle of champagne. She felt a little nap would do her good and clear her brain. She was not to wake until late in the evening, long after the London coach had left, and so was able to persuade herself that fate had taken the matter out of her hands.

Hannah climbed inside the coach at six and Benjamin joined the outside passengers on the roof. The day had turned mellow and fine, turning the cobbles of the twisting streets to pure gold. Sea-gulls wheeled and screamed overhead as the coach rumbled off. The other passengers consisted of a clerk, dressed in a showy waistcoat and, over it, a velvet coat which was rather short in the sleeve and showed a large expanse of dirty cuff; a fat and fussy woman who kept peering suspiciously at the other passengers and clutching a large wicker basket on her lap; a large and rubicund farmer in creaking new boots and a shirt so cruelly starched it was a wonder it did not creak as well; a thin, cross-looking woman with finicking genteel mannerisms whom Hannah privately damned as a governess or some other upper servant; and a school-boy eating sweets from a sticky bag and gazing morosely all around as if hating the whole pernicious race of adults.

New straw had been thrown on the floor on top of the old straw, which had not been cleaned out. Hannah plucked fretfully at bits of straw clinging to her gown and wondered how Lady Beatrice would fare with Lord Alistair.

Usually Hannah's journey home to London was spent in dreaming happily of seeing Sir George Clarence again and rehearsing what she would tell him. But now the shadow of the beautiful Lady Beatrice fell over all. Why had she, Hannah Pym, so recklessly promised to spend the rest of her life with Lady Beatrice? Lady Beatrice did not need her. By the time she sold her horses, her carriage, and her jewels, there would be enough to keep her in modest comfort for the rest of her life.

And why, thought Hannah, had she herself decided to move next year, when her travels were over, to some poky cottage in some rustic village? Surely only a pastoral poet could find comfort in antique Tudor houses with dry rot in the beams and rising damp in the walls. When Hannah had thought of that cottage before, in her mind it had always been summer, with flowers blooming in the garden, roses tumbling over the door, and pleasant bucolic villagers stopping at the garden gate to pass the time of day. Now she thought of a cottage in the winter: of going to bed at six to spare candles, of being snowed up, of being cold and lonely. Her new odd station in life would mean that she would be above the majority of the villagers socially but below the gentry, rather in the position of a governess who belonged to neither the one class nor the other. She and Lady Beatrice would probably murder each other out of sheer boredom. She could not expect a young man like Benjamin to stay away from the city for long.

Her curiosity in her fellow passengers was dimmed because of worries about her own future. Nor did she look for adventures. The only adventure Hannah Pym wanted now was to sit beside her best tea-service, dispensing tea to Sir George, but without Lady Beatrice. She tried to think hopefully of the possible result of Lady Beatrice and Lord Alistair travelling together, but could not. Lord Alistair would no doubt opt to drive his cattle himself and Lady Beatrice would travel alone inside the coach. I should have stayed with them, thought Hannah. I could perhaps have engineered some accident or some diversion to throw them together.

* * *

Before the coach had even left Brighton, Lady Beatrice was pacing agitatedly up and down her drawing-room, the letter Hannah had left for her in her hands. Hannah's message had been brief, almost curt. She liked the Flying Machines and preferred to travel that way. She would call on Lady Beatrice in London and do the best she could to manage that lady's affairs.

Lady Beatrice realized that she had taken Hannah Pym's friendship for granted. She wondered now how she could have been so ungrateful. Without Hannah's strength, she never would have had the courage to defy her parents. Now that Hannah had shown her the road to take, she certainly did not need her. She could live very comfortably in a quiet way from the money she could raise from the sale of her jewels. But the tone of Hannah's short letter seemed to indicate the spinster might be having second thoughts about sharing her life with her, and that came as a rude shock.

The house was empty. The servants had all gone ahead to London. What if Sir Geoffrey had called again to find her unprotected? Had Hannah not considered that possibility?

There was a loud knock at the street door. She automatically waited for some servant to go and answer it before realizing she would need to go down herself.

Lord Alistair stood on the threshold. Behind him stood a magnificent travelling carriage, the one that Benjamin had longed to travel in, with a coachman on the box, two grooms on the backstrap, and two outriders.

'You had better come inside a moment, my lord,' said Lady Beatrice.

He followed her into the shadowy hall and they both stood under the chandelier, which was wrapped up in a bag of holland cloth.

'Miss Pym has decided not to travel with us,' said Lady Beatrice. 'She has taken the six o'clock coach.'

'How strange!' Lord Alistair looked down at her curiously. 'Did you offend her in any way?'

'Not that I know of. Do not look so downcast. I can easily catch the coach.'

Lady Beatrice looked miserable. 'The fact that she left without speaking to me leads me to believe that she regrets our friendship. I must confess I did not realize up until now how much it meant to me. If you can bear my undiluted company, my lord, I think it would be more tactful to leave Miss Pym to her own devices.'

He found he was sorry for her. He thought she looked young and defenceless, and yet surely, after the hell of her marriage, she should be hardened to a minor irritation like the possible loss of a friend. And yet, he thought, when had Lady Beatrice had any friends? He had seen her in saloon or ballroom, always beautiful, always icy, always composed.

'Have you eaten?' he asked.

She looked up at him, puzzled, and then her face cleared and she said with a little laugh, 'Not since breakfast.'

'Then I suggest my servants wait for us until we dine at the Ship, and then we will be on our road. I always get the blue devils when I am hungry.'

At the Ship, always the most popular hostelry in Brighton, a table was miraculously found for them at the bay window. About them rose the buzz and chatter of the other diners, mostly fashionable. The unfashionable still dined at two in the afternoon, the medium fashionable at four, and the very fashionable at around seven.

Lady Beatrice was wearing a pretty little hat tilted slightly over her dark curls. Her close-fitting carriage gown of dark-green velvet flattered her figure, and long pearl earrings complemented the whiteness of her skin.

After they had been served, Lord Alistair said, 'Are you sure you will be able to settle down with Miss Pym and forgo all the pleasures of a social life?'

She smiled ruefully. 'I should be grateful to be free of Sir Geoffrey and my parents, but I confess I am a trifle worried. Miss Pym talks of enlivening our evenings by doing good works, and why not? I have led a shamelessly selfish life.'

'Do not be too hard on yourself,' he said, signalling to the waiter to refill their wineglasses. 'Marriage to Blackstone can hardly have been a bed of roses.'

She turned her glass this way and that and said in a low voice, 'It was disgusting, although easier in recent years, for he would return home usually drunk and unconscious, and then, as soon as he recovered, he would be off gambling and drinking again.' She coloured slightly. Both were aware she had referred obliquely to the fact that Mr Blackstone had usually been too drunk to demand his marital rights.

'But I shall come about,' she said with a slight smile. 'Miss Pym will see to that. Let us talk about you for a change. How is it you have escaped marriage for so long?'

His eyes narrowed slightly as he looked at her, wondering if Lady Beatrice was beginning to flirt with him, but her eyes were still sad.

'I enjoy my bachelor life too much,' he said lightly. 'And I am become very agricultural of late. I own estates in Wiltshire. Good land now, but it was in a shocking state when I got it. At first I hired estate managers to put the land in good heart. The first few were useless and lazy and so I began to study and try to make the changes myself. It became absorbing and interesting. I shall never forget that first good harvest . . . But I must be boring you!'

'Not at all. Do go on.'

'It was a bumper harvest. I was so excited, like a schoolboy, I had to help bring it in myself. Then we had a great harvest party. What dancing! What celebration! It made Almack's on assembly night seem a desert of boredom. Each year, I spend longer there, and each year I become more reluctant to leave.'

'What is your house called? What is it like?'

'Clarendon Park. It was the Davenants' old place. Colonel Davenant died a while back, if you remember. As a younger son, I found myself with capital from prize money gained during my military service but no property, and so I bought it. It is a fine old house, completely Tudor with great chimneys, dark smoky halls, and mullioned windows. There is a fine park and some good natural vistas, but no mock temples or ornamental lakes; nothing to look at but the deer flitting through the trees of the Holm Wood.'

Lady Beatrice leaned slightly back in her chair and half closed her eyes. 'Is it peaceful?' she asked.

He laughed. 'Nothing to listen to on a wet day but the rain dripping down the chimneys. In fact, I think I shall only spend a few days in London before going there. I adore the place.'

'It sounds very pleasant.' Lady Beatrice sighed. 'That Gothic castle in which I was brought up could hardly be called a home. So huge, so bleak, so menacing. I spent my youth in the east wing with my governess and I hardly ever saw my parents.'

He felt an odd desire to protect her. He tried to imagine her at Clarendon Park and could not. But yet, the Lady Beatrice he could not imagine at Clarendon Park was the Lady Beatrice of the ballroom, not the sad and subdued beauty facing him across the table. He began to talk lightly of Brighton society until he had the pleasure of seeing her face relax, and by the time they took their places in his coach, they were on easy, friendly terms. He had meant to travel on the box so as to observe the conventions, but Lady Beatrice was a widow, not a young miss, and so he decided there would be no harm in travelling in her company. He thought briefly of Hannah Pym and wondered what had caused that unpredictable spinster to decide to take the stage-coach.

Hannah was beginning to wonder that very thing herself. The coach was cold and musty. Usually she would have ordered hot bricks for her feet at the first inn they stopped at, but she felt sapped of energy, an unusual state of affairs. She slowly fell asleep, her head jolting with the motion of the coach. She dreamt she was floating in a warm blue sea. She was completely naked. Sir George Clarence was swimming towards her. He was naked as well, and it seemed the most natural thing in the world.

A commotion awoke her. The passengers were screaming. She sat up, blinked, and looked around. The clerk opposite was whey-faced. 'Highwaymen,' he said through white lips and put his fob-watch in his boot for safety. The thin spinster was praying volubly and the farmer was cursing and the woman holding the basket was weeping copiously. The schoolboy seemed unmoved, as if highwaymen were just another part of the adult world he so detested.

The door of the carriage was jerked open and a masked figure stood there, the light from the carriage lamp shining on the barrel of the long horse-pistol he brandished.

'Out, all of you!' he barked.

Shivering and crying and cursing, the passengers climbed down. 'Any interference,' shouted the highwayman to the passengers, coachman, and guard on the roof, 'and I'll shoot this lot.'

Then he glared at the passengers. 'Is this the lot of you?' he demanded.

The thin spinster fell to her knees and babbled, 'Spare me. I have nothing. Nothing!'

He ignored her. He reached out and caught hold of Hannah's arm and pulled her away from the others. 'Get on board,' he ordered the rest of the passengers. They did just that, not one seeming to care for Hannah's plight, except Benjamin, who slid quietly down from the roof of the coach on the far side where the highwayman could not see him and crept off into the darkness.

The coachman cracked his whip and the coach rumbled off, leaving Hannah and the highwayman standing on the road together.

'Well, Sir Geoffrey,' said Hannah quietly, for she had recognized him despite his mask, 'you may stop the charade and release me now.'

He shook her arm furiously. 'Where is she?'

Hannah looked at him levelly. A small bright moon riding high above silvered the landscape, and the wind from the far-away sea moaned across the downs. 'If you mean Lady Beatrice, Sir Geoffrey, she left for London earlier today escorted by Lord Alistair.' Hannah had no intention of telling him that Lady Beatrice had probably left at the same time as the coach in case he managed to ride ahead and catch up with them – that is, if they were ahead. Hannah thought they might have passed the coach while she was asleep.

'It's all your fault, you crook-nosed bag,' he growled. 'You stopped my marriage. You caused my humiliation, and b'Gad, you shall pay for it.' He hurled her away from him. Hannah staggered and fell to her knees.

'Say your last prayers, Miss Pym,' jeered Sir Geoffrey. He raised the pistol.

Hannah closed her eyes. She thought briefly that she had had a good life. She had not known cold or starvation, and who could ask for more than that?

There was a sickening crack. She felt a great fiery pain in her chest and fell forward.

And then she heard a voice in her ear. 'Modom! Are you all right? It is me, Benjamin.'

She dazedly opened her eyes. Benjamin was stooped over her, a large tree branch in his hand. Sir Geoffrey was stretched out cold by the edge of the road.

'I am shot, Benjamin,' whispered Hannah. 'There was a great pain in my chest.'

'You ha'n't been,' protested Benjamin. 'I hit the bleeding shite wiff all me might afore he pulled the poxy trigger. Do get up, modom.'

Hannah wonderingly felt her chest and looked at her hand in the moonlight. There was no blood. The crack which she had believed to be a pistol shot must have been caused by Benjamin's hitting Sir Geoffrey on the head and the pain had been caused by her imagination. Helped by Benjamin, she staggered to her feet.

'What shall we do with him, modom?'

Before Hannah could answer, a posse of militia came pounding up the road on horseback, their captain at the head. The captain swung himself down from the saddle while his soldiers surrounded the fallen Sir Geoffrey. The coachman had stopped at the nearest town and had reported the highwayman to the authorities.

To the captain's urgent queries, Hannah gave him her name and address and said shakily that she was unharmed. 'The coachman said the felon took you apart from the other passengers,' said the captain. 'Do you know why?'

Hannah cast a sharp look at Benjamin. 'I think he was mad,' she said with a shudder. 'He would have killed me if my brave footman had not struck him on the head.' She had no intention of telling the captain that she had recognized Sir Geoffrey. Let Sir Geoffrey find out what it was like to be treated as a common highwayman.

One of the soldiers had removed Sir Geoffrey's mask. 'Ever seen him before?' demanded the captain. 'I am very faint and weak,' said Hannah feebly. 'And my eyes are not strong enough to make out anything in the night. I would like to go to the nearest town and find a bed for the night.'

'As you will, madam,' said the captain. 'We will be taking this felon to the nearest round-house, which is at Castlefort. We'll put you up on a horse and have you there in no time.'

But Hannah could not ride, and so Benjamin mounted and held her in front of him as they plodded through the darkness. 'Why did you not tell that captain about Sir Geoffrey?' asked Benjamin.

'Sir Geoffrey's name would impress them. He will of course say he did it all as a joke. Give him a little while to suffer.'

They reached an inn at Castlefort called the Green Tree. The captain arrived at the same time to explain their luggageless presence to the landlord. Then he saluted smartly and said he would call on them again as soon as the highwayman was safely under lock and key.

He arrived back again just as they were about to begin supper.

'This 'ere highwayman,' said the captain, scratching his powdered wig, 'says as how he is Sir Geoffrey Handford.'

'I know Sir Geoffrey,' said Hannah, affecting amazement. 'These highwaymen are bold rascals. They would say anything.'

'He is demanding to see you, Miss Pym. He says it was all a joke and that he was foxed. He is begging you not to press charges.'

'I have suffered too much to face this creature this night,' said Hannah, putting a hand to her brow in a gesture worthy of the great tragic actress Mrs Siddons. 'I shall call at the round-house at, say, eleven o'clock tomorrow morning.'

'Let him rot,' said Hannah cheerfully to Benjamin after the captain had gone. 'A night in the round-house will do him good. You are a good and brave lad, Benjamin, but if you want to be a good footman, you must realize you are being allowed to sit at table with me because the circumstances are unusual.'

'Yes, modom,' said Benjamin with a grin and sank his knife into the steaming crust of a large steak-and-kidney pie.

Lord Alistair Munro's travelling coach bowled smoothly along. For a good part of the journey, he and Lady Beatrice had chatted amiably, but as the miles flew past and London approached, both fell silent.

How simple it would be to take her in my arms, thought Lord Alistair. But all that would do would be to hand her another scalp for her belt. He eyed her coldly, and in the light of the carriage lamp Lady Beatrice caught that look and turned her head bleakly away. Why, he despises me still, she thought. Even Miss Pym has taken me in dislike.

How exhilarated she had been when she had first won her freedom! But now life stretched out dull and empty, and lifeless to the grave.

A hard sore lump was rising in her throat. She tried to fight it down. A pathetic little sob was wrung from her, and to her own horror, large tears welled up in her eyes and spilled down her cheeks.

'What is the matter?' cried Lord Alistair. He leaned forward and took her head gently in his long fingers and turned her face towards his, looking with amazement at the large tears rolling unchecked down her cheeks.

'Y-you d-do not like me,' whispered Lady Beatrice.

'Beatrice! What can I say? I am terrified of you. I fear one move, one sign of warmth from me would set you laughing at me. You must know you have a bad reputation as a flirt.'

She took out a handkerchief and blew her nose and looked blindly at him. 'That was when I was so hurt, so furious at what life had done to me. I thought all men like Blackstone, greedy and cruel and lustful.'

He wrapped his arms around her and drew her against his chest, holding her gently like a child.

'Do not cry,' he said. 'All that is over now.'

Her lips trembled and he bent his head and kissed her slowly and firmly, then deeper, then with rousing passion as her body was rocked against his own by the motion of the coach.

Never had Lady Beatrice thought to feel passion for any man, or any such burning sweetness as this. Her body now craved the intimacies which had once disgusted her.

He freed his lips and said sadly, 'If only you could find it in your heart to love me.'

'But I do!' cried Lady Beatrice. 'That is the tragedy of it all!'

He gave a laugh of sheer relief and gladness. 'That, my sweeting, is the comedy of it all. I love you and you love me and we have been wasting so much time. Kiss me again!'

And so she did and went on returning hot sweet languorous kisses until the carriage began to rattle over the cobbles of London and she had shyly promised to be his bride.

'I now worry about what to say to Miss Pym,' she

said. 'Will she be very angry that I am not to live with her after all?'

'Let me tell you, my love, that that managing spinster has already told me we should both suit, and I have no doubt in my mind now that she deliberately left us to travel alone in the hope that something would happen. We shall call on her tomorrow and tell her our news!'

In the morning, Hannah, accompanied by Benjamin, went to the round-house.

Sir Geoffrey looked a sorry figure. He was unshaven and bits of the straw he had been forced to sleep on clung to his clothes.

'Leave us,' said Hannah to the guard. When he had left, she looked sternly at Sir Geoffrey. 'If I press charges against you,' she said, 'you know that you may hang.'

'You could not be so cruel,' he said, all his former bluster gone.

'My dear sir, why not? You tried to kill me.'

He hung his head. 'The pistol was not loaded. You can ask the captain. I was only going to take my revenge by giving you a fright.'

'You nearly frightened me to death,' snapped Hannah, 'and for that alone, you deserve to hang.'

'Please do not do this to me,' he whimpered. 'I will pay you anything . . . anything.'

'Now you're talking sense,' said Benjamin cheerfully.

'Be quiet, Benjamin!' cried Hannah. She sat for a few moments and said slowly, 'I will let you off on one condition.'

'Which is?'

'I want you to write me a full confession of your attempts to abduct Lady Beatrice and give it to me. You must never approach her again. If you do, I shall turn your confession over to the authorities.'

'Anything,' he gabbled eagerly.

Hannah drew several sheets of paper out of her capacious reticule and then sent Benjamin to fetch ink and a quill. Both sat silently while Sir Geoffrey wrote busily.

At last, when he had finished, Hannah took the confession from him and read it carefully. It was ungrammatical and badly spelt, but she knew it would do. She tucked the papers in her reticule and stood up.

'I shall tell the guard I am not pressing charges,' she said severely. 'But should I ever see you so much as speak to Lady Beatrice, I shall take these papers to the nearest magistrate.'

Humbly Sir Geoffrey thanked her. Hannah went off with Benjamin after her and calmly told the captain that Sir Geoffrey had indeed been foxed and had merely been playing a silly and dangerous prank.

'So that's that, Benjamin,' said Hannah. 'We will take the next up coach and we will soon be home.'

'Had enough of travels?' asked Benjamin.

Hannah laughed. 'I have had enough of travels and matchmaking to last me a lifetime. No more stage-coach journeys after this, Benjamin. It's home to London for us!'

8

As false as dicers' oaths.

William Shakespeare

Hannah found she was glad to be back in London among the smells and noise. Her little apartment looked pretty and cosy. She felt she should go and call on Lady Beatrice and find when she planned to move in. They would need to share a bed, a prospect Hannah did not relish. But if only Lady Beatrice would stay away until she had a chance to entertain Sir George Clarence in private, then Hannah felt she could cope with whatever was to come.

She was settling down the following afternoon to enjoy a few moments' leisure after cleaning the rooms and lighting the fire. Benjamin had done all the shopping, but she still could not get it through his head that he was supposed to do the housework as well.

He had begged leave to go out and Hannah did hope he was not gambling again. She dreaded the day when a tearful Benjamin would come to her and say he had lost some vast sum.

There was a knock at the door and her thoughts immediately flew to Sir George. But he would not know of her return, she reflected, as she smoothed down her skirt and went to answer the door.

She stepped back a bit, as if dazzled by the glow of happiness on the faces of the couple who stood on the threshold. Hannah looked at Lady Beatrice and Lord Alistair Munro and held out both her hands in welcome. 'I told you you were both well suited,' she said.

'Well, Matchmaker Pym,' said Lord Alistair when they were all seated before the fire, 'your plan worked. Did you deliberately leave us to travel together?'

'Yes,' said Hannah simply. 'I did so hope something would happen.'

'And so it has,' said Lady Beatrice with a laugh. 'We are to be married by special licence in two weeks' time, and you, Miss Pym, are to be my maid of honour.'

'I shall be delighted,' exclaimed Hannah. 'But you have not heard my news.'

She told them of Sir Geoffrey's dressing as a highwayman to waylay the coach.

'Enough is enough,' said Lord Alistair. 'I shall call him out.'

'No need for that.' Hannah told the amazed couple about Sir Geoffrey's confession.

'You are a miracle worker,' said Lady Beatrice and looked so radiant and so beautiful that Hannah heaved a sigh of relief that such a priceless pearl would not be around to dazzle Sir George.

They talked for a long time, reminiscing about their various adventures in Brighton, and then the couple took their leave.

Hannah did a jig on the hearthrug after they had left. Then she brought out a travelling writing-desk and set it on her lap and began to compose an invitation to Sir George Clarence. Would he be free on the morrow for tea at five o'clock?

Then she waited in a frenzy of impatience for Benjamin to return. When he finally did saunter in, she berated him roundly on his laziness before handing him the letter. 'Ah, Sir George,' said Benjamin with a knowing grin. 'Wondered why you was in such a taking.' He darted out before Hannah could find something to throw at him.

She paced up and down and up and down, waiting for Benjamin's return, and when he did return at last with a letter which said Sir George was pleased to accept Miss Pym's kind invitation, Hannah felt almost sick with nerves.

She hardly slept that night, imagining how he would look and what he would say while getting up to find a suitable gown to wear and then deciding a moment later it would not do at all.

The next morning dragged its weary length along

even though she cleaned everything twice over and tried on several more gowns. The day limped on past two o'clock and then time suddenly began to speed up, moving faster and faster and faster towards the magic hour of five o'clock.

Benjamin was brushed down so many times and so ruthlessly that he said she would wear out his livery.

By ten to five, the cakes and little sandwiches were laid out on a round table before the fire. The silver kettle was steaming on the spirit-stove and a canister of the best tea London could supply was waiting to be opened.

And then there was that knock, and all at once he was there, just as she had imagined him, silver hair brushed and shining, piercing blue eyes resting on her as she told him all about her adventures.

'You are an amazing lady,' he said finally. 'Where do you plan to visit next?'

'I have had my fill of adventures and travel,' said Hannah. 'How are the gardens at Thornton Hall? Has the work on them finished? I would dearly like to see them.'

'Then you must come with us one day,' said Sir George.

Hannah felt suddenly cold. 'Us?' she asked.

He smiled. 'I am afraid, dear friend, that my bachelor days are over. I cannot wait to introduce the lady to you.'

Benjamin stood frozen behind Hannah's chair. Then he put one hand on her shoulder and gripped it hard.

'I should be delighted,' said Hannah in a colourless voice. 'Who is this lady?'

'A Miss Bearcroft.'

'*Miss?*'

He wagged a playful finger at Hannah. 'Ah, Miss Pym, you must think I am snatching a maiden out of the schoolroom. Miss Bearcroft is of mature years. In fact, I took the liberty of asking her to call here to meet you. She should arrive at any moment.'

'More tea?' asked Hannah through dry lips.

'No, I thank you.'

There was a long and awkward silence. Then Hannah asked, 'Are you affianced to this Miss Bearcroft?'

'Not yet. I have still to find the courage. She is so pretty, so gay, and I am afeard she would laugh at an old stick like myself.'

'Tish,' said Hannah, rallying. 'Miss Bearcroft will be the most fortunate of ladies. The door, Benjamin!'

'I didn't hear nothing,' said Benjamin flatly and gripping Hannah's shoulder harder.

'Oh yes, you did,' said Hannah wearily. 'Answer the door.'

Benjamin reluctantly did as he was told and Miss Bearcroft bounced in, followed by her maid. Sir George rose and effected the introductions. Miss Bearcroft offered Hannah two fingers to shake. Hannah ignored the fingers and bowed slightly from the waist.

Miss Bearcroft, although in her thirties, was dressed *à la jeune fille* in sprigged muslin with little puffed sleeves worn under a light pelisse of blue silk trimmed with swansdown. Around her tiny waist was a broad blue satin sash. Her brown hair under a frivolous bonnet was a riot of glossy curls and her pansy-brown eyes were very large and slightly protruding. 'I am tewwibly pleased to meet you, Miss Pym,' she gushed as she sat down. 'I adoah meeting old servants.'

'Now, now,' said Sir George, his face rather pink, 'Miss Pym is a lady of private means.'

Miss Bearcroft's eyes grew rounder. 'But you told me she was your bwother's housekeeper!'

'Those days are gone,' said Sir George. 'I have just been enjoying hearing about Miss Pym's latest adventures. Do tell Miss Bearcroft about meeting the Prince of Wales, Miss Pym.'

Hannah forced a laugh. 'In truth, Sir George, I have talked so much this afternoon. I fear I have given myself the headache. Would you be so good as to excuse me?'

'By all means. Come, Miss Bearcroft.'

'Yes, you must have your west,' lisped Miss Bearcroft, making Hannah feel at least a hundred. 'My old nurse used to get *such* pains in the head. If your son would be so good as to show us out.'

Sir George, who had been regarding his beloved up until that moment with a certain amused indulgence in his blue eyes, stiffened. 'Your wits are wandering,' he said harshly. 'How can *Miss* Pym have a son, and why on earth would she have him dressed in livery?'

Miss Bearcroft's eyes filled with tears. 'Now you are

cwoss with me and I cannot bear it. You know I am just a silly little thing.'

Hannah sank down wearily in her chair after they had gone and waved a tired hand to indicate that Benjamin had permission to sit down as well.

'Fool!' said Hannah harshly.

'And no fool like an old fool,' agreed Benjamin.

'Meaning me?'

'O' course not. Meaning Sir George. No wonder she ain't been married afore, and I'll tell you something else, mum – that there Miss Bearcroft ain't no better than she should be.'

'Come, Benjamin. I am grateful for your attempted moral support, but despite her bitchiness and silliness, she is all that is proper.' Hannah lay back and half closed her eyes. 'I remember there was a friend of the Clarences', a guest ... what was his name? Ah, Churchill. Mr Churchill. A fine upstanding man, very clever, very elegant. Forty-eight if he was a day. He fell in love with a silly vulgar chit. Mrs Clarence tried all in her power to dissuade him, but he would have none of it. He married the girl.'

'And lived unhappily ever after,' commented Benjamin gloomily.

'Oh, no, he remained delighted with her and laughed uproariously at all her silliness. She was a constant delight to him. It has always amazed me how gentlemen prefer very silly women. It is what they expect us to be.'

'But this Mrs Churchill was surely just silly, not vicious,' asked Benjamin.

'No, she was not vicious,' said Hannah slowly.

'There you are. I'm telling you, modom, it's your duty to find out about this Miss Bearcroft and put him wise.'

'Sir George is nothing to do with me. He has made his own bed. Let him lie on it.'

Benjamin tried to protest, but Hannah reminded him sharply of his duties as a footman and commanded him to take away the tea-things and wash them. She was going to bed.

The footman anxiously watched her go to her bedroom and slam the door. When had the redoubtable Miss Pym ever felt the need to lie down during the day? Benjamin busied himself about his duties while his brain worked furiously. There must be some way Sir George could be made to see the folly of his ways.

Lady Beatrice was surprised next morning to hear that a person called Benjamin Stubbs was demanding an audience with her.

'I do not know any person called Stubbs,' said Lady Beatrice. 'What sort of fellow is he?'

'Footman, my lady,' said the servant. 'Tall chap in black livery.'

'Ah,' said Lady Beatrice, remembering Hannah's servant was called Benjamin, 'I think I had better see him. Show him up.'

'Is anything wrong with Miss Pym?' asked Lady Beatrice anxiously as Benjamin was ushered in.

'Everythink's wrong, my lady,' said Benjamin gloomily.

'Lord Alistair Munro,' announced Lady Beatrice's footman from the doorway.

'You are come at the right time,' said Lady Beatrice, running to meet him. 'Here is Miss Pym's Benjamin and something has happened to her.'

Lord Alistair's face darkened. 'Not Sir Geoffrey! Don't tell me he has harmed her.'

'No, no,' protested Benjamin. 'Nuffink like that. It's that there Sir George Clarence.'

Lady Beatrice frowned in puzzlement and then her face cleared. 'Ah, I have it. The brother of her late employer.'

'The same,' said Benjamin gloomily. 'Miss Pym was in high alt because Sir George was coming to tea. Seems he allus visits her after one of her journeys because he likes hearing about her adventures. Well, the mistress was in such a taking, dressing up in one gown and changing it for another and cleaning and cleaning until everything shone like glass. In comes Sir George and it all looks April and May and he can't seem to hear enough of her tales. Then he ups and says he's about to get married or rather pop the question to a Miss Bearcroft, and he has asked this Miss Bearcroft to call round and meet Miss Pym.'

'Men!' said Lady Beatrice.

'So in comes this Miss Bearcroft all lisps and giggles and mutton dressed as lamb and *she offers Miss Pym two fingers to shake*. But there's worse. As she was leaving, for Miss Pym said she had the headache, and no wonder if you ask me, this poxy trollop having already referred to Miss Pym as an old servant, she ups and asks Miss Pym to ask her *son* to show them out. Sir George goes all frosty, as if he's just realized the mistake he's about to make, but Miss Pym, and she's very wise, she says gentlemen like fools and more or less says he'll probably be very happy. And then she goes off to bed and it not even bedtime, and her eyes this morning are all red like she's been crying and I can't bear it.' Benjamin took out a large grubby handkerchief and blew his nose.

Lady Beatrice spread her hands in a gesture of helplessness. 'I do not really see what we can do.'

'Well, you see, Miss Pym don't agree with me,' said Benjamin earnestly, 'but I think this here Miss Bearcroft is Haymarket ware, and if you could find out and if he was put wise, like, the mistress could be happy again.'

'You are a very loyal servant, Benjamin,' said Lord Alistair. 'Are you sure you are not romancing?'

'I can tell a lightskirt a mile off,' said Benjamin. 'No matter how they's dressed.'

'I will see what I can find out,' said Lord Alistair slowly, 'but I cannot hold out much hope.'

When Benjamin had left, he turned to Lady Beatrice and said, 'What do you think? Should I waste time I might be spending with you finding out about Benjamin's trollop?'

'Oh, please do something,' begged Lady Beatrice. 'I always used to think Miss Pym too bossy and dictatorial, but I would rather she stayed that way, for I love her dearly.'

'Then I will do it for you, my sweet, but kiss me first!'

Their kisses were so long and so intense that Lord Alistair forgot all about Miss Pym's predicament and would have gladly continued to forget about it had Lady Beatrice not at last freed herself and said in a ragged voice, 'I think you should go before we both forget we are not yet married. Do try to do something for Miss Pym.'

Lord Alistair first called on the formidable Countess Lieven, one of the patronesses of Almack's. To his inquiries, the countess said she had never heard of Miss Bearcroft and she had certainly never even applied for vouchers to the famous assembly rooms. From there he went to his club and questioned all he met and at last elicited the news that Miss Bearcroft had lately arrived from India and was being sponsored by Lady Beauclerc. Lord Alistair raised his thin eyebrows in surprise. Lady Beauclerc was a grasping harridan who would thrust anyone on society provided she was paid enough money to do so.

'India,' mused Lord Alistair. 'Where do I go for gossip now? The military or the East India Company?' He tossed a coin and it came down in favour of the East India Company.

He made his way over to the City and asked to see Sir Miles Burford, one of the directors. It was the only name he could remember. An old clerk asked him to be seated. He came back and said Sir Miles would see Lord Alistair as soon as possible.

Lord Alistair waited and waited. The clerk served him tea. The hands of the yellow-faced clock on the office wall crept slowly round.

'Is he very busy?' Lord Alistair asked the clerk. 'Or does he like to keep people waiting?'

'Sir Miles likes to keep people waiting, my lord, no matter what their consequence,' said the old clerk with a trace of venom. 'He feels it adds to his consequence.' A bell rang in the inner office. 'Sir Miles will see you now,' said the clerk, and shuffled to open the door.

Sir Miles was a portly man, his heavy face hanging down pear-shaped under a small wig perched on top of his head.

'Sit down, Lord Alistair,' he said pompously, 'and let me know how I may serve you.'

'It is a delicate matter,' said Lord Alistair. 'I am trying to find out about a certain Miss Bearcroft.'

Sir Miles placed his podgy hands on the desk and heaved himself up. 'I do not wish to insult you, my lord, but I am a busy man and have no time to waste talking about ladies of whom I have never heard. Good day to you!'

'It was a civil question,' said Lord Alistair. 'I would remind you I own a considerable amount of shares in the East India Company.'

Sir Miles forced a smile. 'Of course, of course, and if there is anything about the workings of the company you would like to know, we are always at your service.'

'But you have never heard of Miss Bearcroft?'

'No. Now, if you will excuse me . . .' He fussily shifted some papers in front of him.

Lord Alistair took his leave. The little old clerk

helped him into his greatcoat and peered up into his face in an oddly inquisitive way. Lord Alistair turned in the doorway. 'I wonder whether, Mr . . . ?'

'Chipping.'

'I wonder whether you have heard at any time, from anyone arriving back from India, of a Miss Bearcroft.'

Mr Chipping looked quickly at the closed door of Sir Miles Burford's office and then laid a chalky finger alongside his nose. 'I go to the chop-house, Brown's, hard by, in five minutes, my lord.' He again glanced at that closed door in a warning way.

'Very well,' said Lord Alistair in a low voice. 'I shall meet you there.'

He went to the chop-house and found a dark corner to sit in while he waited for Mr Chipping. It was much frequented by clerks, all gossiping about stocks and shares and the iniquities of their employers. Mr Chipping sidled in through the crowd and sat down gingerly next to Lord Alistair and looked at him hopefully, like a robin looking for crumbs.

Lord Alistair smiled. 'Shall we say ten guineas?' he asked.

Mr Chipping rubbed his hands gleefully. 'We shall indeed, my lord. We shall indeed. Now this Miss Philadelphia Bearcroft came on the London Season back in the late eighties, but she did not take. Father was a colonel, dead this age, mother pushing and ambitious. Decides to take daughter out to India in the hope of catching some homesick prize of an officer for her daughter. Now we comes to Sir Miles's brother, James.'

'Do we indeed. You intrigue me.'

'Oh, it's a real ten guineas' worth.

'Mr James Burford is another of the directors of the company, based in Calcutta. I was out there until the climate nigh killed me. Mr Burford has a marvellous mansion, plenty of money, unlimited power, and a little faded sort of lady of a wife and ten children. He meets Miss Bearcroft at a ball and is smitten. They tried to keep it quiet, but it soon became known that Miss Bearcroft had become the mistress of Mr James, and she lorded it over the wives of the employees of the East India Company and they had to be nice to her or Mr James might have sent their husbands packing. Finally the flighty Miss Bearcroft got too much for some of them and a deputation of the ladies went to see Mrs Burford. No one could have believed that downtrodden lady would have shown such strength of character. Gossip has it that she upped and told her husband that unless he got rid of this Miss Bearcroft, she, Mrs Burford, would make such a scandal in the courts asking for a divorce that he would never be able to hold up his head again in polite society. So he settled a vast sum on this Miss Bearcroft and then got her a passage home.'

'Wonderful!' said Lord Alistair. 'You have earned your ten guineas.'

Sir George Clarence sat uneasily on a striped satin sofa in Lady Beauclerc's drawing-room, with Miss Bearcroft beside him. Lady Beauclerc had left them alone together and gone out and shut the door behind her. It was too much for the conventional Sir George. No gentleman should be alone in a room with an unmarried lady and with the door closed. He went up and opened it wide and then sat down again.

Miss Bearcroft looked at him coyly over her fan. 'I decleah you are cwoss with me still.'

'I am a little,' said Sir George reluctantly. 'Miss Pym is a very dear friend and a most unusual lady. As a friend of mine, you should have offered her your whole hand, nor should you have made that ridiculous remark about her footman being her son.'

'But what else was I to think?' pleaded Miss Bearcroft. 'I mean, she's only a servant. What is she doing with a servant herself?'

'It's a long story, but do realize this, and then I will say no more on the matter. Whatever status Miss Pym held in the past, she is now a gentlewoman and I would thank you to remember it.'

Behind the shelter of her fan, Miss Bearcroft's face hardened as her mind worked furiously. Yes, she had been jealous of that stupid crooked-nosed creature because Miss Pym and Sir George had looked so comfortable together. And yet, what had she to fear from such as Hannah Pym?

She gave a tinkling little laugh and lowered her fan. 'In truth, I was jeawous,' she lisped.

'Jealous? Of Miss Pym?'

'Oh, I know it is ridiculous. But you are so careful of the conventions when you are with me but think nothing of being closeted alone with Miss Pym in her apartment. I shall make amends. I would love to hear her tell of her adventures and I shall become her friend, too.'

Sir George hesitated. Somewhere at the back of his brain a little alarm bell was beginning to sound. Only that morning, a friend of his had told him that Lady Beauclerc was a thruster of the unfashionable on society. He remembered how he had met both Miss Bearcroft and Lady Beauclerc. He had been leaving his house and Miss Bearcroft had let out a cry and stumbled against him. She said she had twisted her ankle. Lady Beauclerc had eagerly accepted Sir George's offer to escort them both home and had pressed him to stay to tea and then had left them together.

And yet he felt he had somehow to make amends to Hannah Pym.

'I will send a servant to her and suggest we call together tomorrow,' he said.

'And you will see how charming I can be!' cried Miss Bearcroft.

Benjamin called on Lord Alistair the following day and learned with great satisfaction of Miss Bearcroft's background. 'I did not tell Miss Pym,' said Lord Alistair, 'for I thought it better to tell you first and leave it to you to break the news to her. She may decide to do nothing. She is a shrewd lady and may know that a gentleman often blames the very person who makes the scales fall from his eyes.'

The footman thought about that as he made his way to South Audley Street. He knew that Sir George and

Miss Bearcroft were to call that afternoon. Hannah had at first said she would not see them and then had changed her mind. Benjamin said nothing to Hannah but helped to arrange the tea-things. There was no air of excitement and Hannah was wearing a plain gown of green velvet, although it was of good cut and went well with her sandy-coloured hair.

This time Miss Bearcroft startled her by embracing her warmly. Hannah replied by detaching herself as quickly as possible and ushering the couple into chairs.

As tea was dispensed, Miss Bearcroft said with every appearance of eagerness, 'I am all agog to hear your adventures, Miss Pym.'

Before Hannah could speak, Benjamin gave tongue. 'Ain't nothing compared to yourn, Miss Bearcroft.'

'I beg your pardon,' said Sir George frostily. 'Besides, I thought you were deaf and dumb, you jackanapes. I thought there was something wrong when I heard you speak the other day.'

'Oh, that is another story,' said Hannah with terrible false gaiety. 'It all happened–'

'In India,' finished Benjamin gleefully.

'Benjamin!' roared Hannah. 'Have you taken leave of your senses? I have never been to India.'

Benjamin grinned insolently. 'But you have, ha'n't you, Miss Bearcroft?'

'Well, really,' exclaimed Miss Bearcroft. 'We should leave now, Sir George. Miss Pym has been a servant and that may be why she cannot keep her own in his place.'

'And why can't you keep yours?' jeered Benjamin. 'Miss Pym is a lady and I don't like to see my mistress making tea for the demi-monde.'

Sir George stood up. 'Explain yourself now,' he demanded.

'Well, sir,' said Benjamin, turning all meek and humble, 'it's a well-known fact that Miss Bearcroft here was the mistress o' Mr James Burford o' the East India Company for years.'

Sir George's blue gaze fell on Miss Bearcroft. Her face was contorted with fury. 'Damn you!' she whispered.

'So,' went on Benjamin unrepentantly, 'it goes against the grain to see my mistress having to take insults from the likes o' you, the camel o' Calcutta, allus getting humped.'

Miss Bearcroft leaped to her feet and threw the contents of her teacup full into Benjamin's face and then ran from the apartment. There was a shocked silence.

Then Sir George collected his hat and stick and said in a strangled voice, 'Good day to both of you.'

'No,' pleaded Hannah, 'you must not go. Benjamin has run mad. He will apologize.' Her eyes filled with tears.

Sir George sat down again and looked at the floor. 'You had better tell me all, young man,' he said. And so Benjamin did, in a quiet voice, casting worried looks all the time at Hannah.

'You see,' finished Benjamin, 'I had to find out. Miss Pym knew none of this, nor would she have let me say a thing if she did, but I could not stand by and see you gulled, sir.'

'I am an old fool,' said Sir George quietly, 'and I should be thankful to you. Indeed, I am thankful to you. I was already coming to the conclusion I had made a sad mistake. I do not go about in the world as often as I used to. That is no doubt why Lady Beauclerc considered me easy prey for her protégée. But if you care so much for the sensitivity of your mistress, Benjamin, then I suggest that in future you do not use the language of the gutter in front of her.'

Benjamin hung his head.

'Leave us, Benjamin,' said Hannah quietly.

Benjamin shuffled out.

Hannah turned to Sir George. 'I am so very sorry,' she said softly. 'You must think that association with such as I has made you the butt of that sort of coarseness.'

He raised a white hand in protest. 'It was strong medicine, I admit. When did he find his voice?'

'Ah, that,' said Hannah, carefully pouring him a cup of tea. 'Did I not tell you? Well . . .'

Benjamin leaned against the door of his room, anxiously biting his knuckles, listening to the rise and fall of voices until he slowly began to relax.

'And so,' said Sir George when he finally rose to leave, 'do you go on more travels, Miss Pym?'

Hannah thought quickly. She did not want to stay in London now, waiting and hoping to see him. Better to go away for a little again until he was completely recovered from Miss Bearcroft. She made up her mind.

'I shall go to Dover,' she said, 'and I shall see the sea again.'

'And when do you go?'

'Soon. After the wedding of Lady Beatrice. I am to be maid of honour,' said Hannah proudly.

He rose to leave and she looked at him a little sadly, wondering if they would ever be on their own easy footing again. He paused in the doorway. 'I have just remembered. You were anxious to see the gardens at Thornton Hall, were you not? I will drive you there tomorrow if the weather holds fine.'

Hannah thanked him shyly. Inside his bedroom, where he had been listening all the while, Benjamin rolled on his bed and kicked his heels in the air and crowed with sheer relief.

The wedding of Lady Beatrice and Lord Alistair Munro was a quiet affair, with only Hannah as maid of honour and a friend of Lord Alistair's as brideman to see them joined in marriage. Hannah cried copiously and loudly all through the wedding service and enjoyed herself immensely. The foursome had a wedding breakfast at an inn near the church. Hannah, unusually for her, became rather tipsy and only Benjamin knew it was caused more by sheer happiness than alcohol. For Hannah had not only visited the gardens at Thornton Hall with Sir George but had taken a drive with him at the fashionable hour in Hyde Park. And he had urged her to call on him again as soon as she reached London after her next adventure and had said that he would take her to Vauxhall Pleasure Gardens.

'So,' said Lord Alistair when he was alone with Lady Beatrice in his town house where they were to spend their first night together, 'who knows – we may soon be attending Miss Pym's wedding.'

'I would like to think so,' said Lady Beatrice. 'But Miss Pym did let fall that Sir George now regards her in the light of an old friend and Miss Pym thinks gentlemen never fall in love with their lady friends.'

'You mean hate is more akin to love than friendship?'

'So Miss Pym would have it.'

'And are you happy to be spending the rest of your days with me rather than Miss Pym?'

She looked up at him teasingly. 'Instead of asking me about Hannah Pym, why do you not leave me so that my maid can undress me.'

He gazed into her eyes and then said in a ragged voice, 'Let me be your maid.'

She raised her arms above her head and said gently, 'By all means.'

In a very short time, Hannah Pym, the matchmaker who had brought them together, was forgotten as they tumbled over each other in a frenzy of love-making.

A few streets away, Hannah closed her Bible and put it beside the bed and composed herself for sleep. Her thoughts turned to Lady Beatrice and Lord Alistair and then jumped away like a scalded cat. Best not to think what they were doing. Better to look forward to that journey to Dover, and then perhaps end her travels for once and for all.